I0635767

The

Orange
Hangover

A novel

Rahul Saini

JAICO PUBLISHING HOUSE

Ahmedabad Bangalore Bhopal Bhubaneswar Chennai
Delhi Hyderabad Kolkata Lucknow Mumbai

Published by Jaico Publishing House
A-2 Jash Chambers, 7-A Sir Phirozshah Mehta Road
Fort, Mumbai - 400 001
jaicopub@jaicobooks.com
www.jaicobooks.com

THE ORANGE HANGOVER
ISBN 978-81-8495-302-2

First Jaico Impression: 2012
Fourth Jaico Impression: 2012

Printed by

When you grow up, your heart dies.

– Allison Reynolds, *The Breakfast Club* (1985)

For Gabru Chotta Kutta Jawan

From : superna_super_super@lmail.com

To : rishabhhappy247@allmail.com

Date : Friday, April 25, 2011 at 7:11 PM

Subject : I don't know.

Rishabh, I have been meaning to say this for a long time now. It's more difficult for me to say this than it is for you to know. Since I came here, we both have been struggling to keep our relationship alive. We can either keep lying to each other (and ourselves) about it forever, or we can face the truth that things are not working out for us. It breaks my heart to say this, but we need to accept the fact that our relationship is over. Things are never gonna be the same again – we are never gonna be *the way we were* again.

I wish you all the happiness and all the luck for everything in your life. Thank you for being a part of my life.

Love,

Superna

What? Is she implying that this is a break-up note? There is *no way* I am gonna accept this. This relationship is *not* over. It's only a rough patch that we are going through and she knows that too. Otherwise why would she sign it as 'Love, Superna.' She still very much loves me. And I am gonna set everything right – it's just a matter of time.

Part 1

It's not a lie!

I did not get fired; I quit. And I am not even lying. It is so, so not true that I was fired and can't get another job. That is *not* why I am leaving this town and going back to my hometown, no matter what everyone around me may think. And neither is this any kind of defense mechanism of mine. Yes, I totally was the one who quit the job. Well, it was not exactly quitting, it was more like... circumstantial. Wait a minute, what am I saying? *It was quitting.* God! My life is so over! This was such a great place and I used to have so much fun.

My train of thought runs faster than the train I am travelling in right now. I am being forced to go back to my hometown after spending a good eight years in Gurgaon because of, what you could call, a set of unfortunate events. But I must not let this whole thing affect me so bad – I must distract myself. I look around in the train compartment. My Mom is still sleeping on the chair next to mine and she is a sound sleeper. She won't wake up even if I start screaming and dancing around her.

The train comes to a halt and I am not interested in knowing what station we have reached. I just hope that an interesting co-passenger occupies the vacant seat next to me.

I look at the door of the coach and I see a guy come in with a bag in his hand. It's a weird thing isn't it? At times some people look so familiar when you have never even seen them before. There is something about this guy's face that looks familiar for sure. As he comes and sits next to me, I try real hard to remember whom he reminds me of but in vain.

After sitting there in silence for a few seconds, I decide to strike up a conversation.

"Hi," I turn to him and say, "You really remind me of someone."

He turns to me, smiles and says, "Rishabh Suri."

"No, that's my name. That's not who you remind me of..."

Wait a minute, how does he know my name? Is he a spy? But then again, why would a spy be interested in me? Maybe he just noticed my name on the reservation chart outside and remembered it. Or maybe *his* name is Rishabh Suri too and he is only introducing himself.

"Abhinav, from Saint Joseph's," he says.

I look at him more carefully this time. Yes, that's who he resembles. It's him. God! He has grown *fat*. He used to be so skinny back in school.

"Hey! I knew it was you. So nice to see you," I say.

"How are you?" he asks.

"Good. What's up these days? Where are you? It's so good to see you after all this time."

"Things have been really great," he says. "After school I went to

IIT Delhi. Four years there and then I worked in Mumbai for a year. After that I went to IIM Ahmedabad. Now I am working in California." He says all this as if studying at all these places and working abroad has made him a greater person. I don't like his tone. Now I actually do remember him from school. He was always this cocky and I was never fond of him. He was terrible at literature and I remember sitting with him for endless hours and helping him with Shakespeare. He would never get it. 'Why do they talk this way? Why can't they say *you* instead of *thee* like normal people do? How come no one can see that Portia is a girl?' he would always ask.

"Just came back from the US last week. Actually I am here to promote my book," he says and looks at me. Then he lets out a little laugh and says, "Yeah, I wrote a book too." He takes a pause to see my reaction. I give him none and he continues, "I was in Delhi for the promotion and all, you know how it is, the media, the events. It's so tiring."

"That is great. Congratulations," I say.

"Thank you," he nods.

"I just stayed for a day in Panipat to get away from all the madness," he says.

Oh, so it was Panipat – the station.

"That is great," I say, "so you are on your way to Jalandhar now?"

"No, actually I will be getting off at Ambala."

"Ok, going there for work or otherwise?"

"My wife is there. She is expecting," he smiles.

Oh my God! He is married and is about to have a kid too!

"Hey! That is great! Congratulations... again."

"Thank you," he nods again.

I smile at him trying to appear all cheerful and happy for him but really speaking, I freak out. How can he be married *and* have children already? *It's so early!* I sit there in silence for a while. How can some people have it all so easy? This person sitting next to me is as old as I am and I have known him for most years of our childhood. Back then our lives were so similar. We used to have the same kind of problems and do the same homework. I used to think that our lives would remain alike forever. But just look at us now – he is all settled in life and sounds so clear about everything, and I have no idea what I want out of my life or where I am heading.

"What are you doing these days?" he asks.

"I studied Architecture after school. Been working in Gurgaon," I say.

"Oh great. So you are going home for a holiday. What firm are you working with?"

"Actually... I am between jobs right now," I hesitate.

"Hmm, with the recession on it must be very tough to hold on to jobs," he says.

Ok, I do not want to talk to him *at all* now. What is he implying? I was not fired, *I quit*!

Wait, ok, I will tell you the whole story as it actually happened and then you guys decide for yourselves whether I was fired or I quit.

Meeting a girl

It all began at the grand farewell party at my friend, Vishal's uncle's farmhouse in Gurgaon. Vishal was going to London for a two-year Post Grad. Degree in Business Administration and the *uncle* was off on a vacation to Europe so his farmhouse was... well, very much available for Vishal to do anything he wanted. (You know how it happens right? You slip a 500 rupee note into the caretaker's pocket and the place is yours for the night.)

It was a cool party. Apart from everything else, the food was beyond awesome. From *pao bhaji* to *chowmein*, we had everything. And the music was great too. The new Black Eyed Peas album *The E.N.D.* had released around that time, so *I gotta feeling (that tonight's gonna be a good night)* was played like seven times over, on request.

I love most kinds of music, but it's just that... I am not a great fan of loud music (or dancing, for that matter). So, armed with one glass of coke, I was soon out of the hall, heading for the garden. Looking around at the garden, I could not resist wondering how much money these rich people have. There was a willow tree next to a small pond and a majestic fountain in the middle of the garden which looked as if it had been transported straight from that famous square in Paris. What was it called – the set of those two fountains? Oh yes, *Fontaines de la Concorde*. It's really insane – the things these people do with their money. I mean, haven't they seen all those pictures and videos of the starving children from Africa that keep circulating on the Internet? There are so many people who need money. But the rich, they just don't care. They erect diamond-studded fountains in their gardens and have... big parties without a thought about the rest of the world.

(Not that the fountain here is diamond studded, or we should not have had *this* particular party – it was totally required. It's just that some people waste their money for no reason.) Anyway, it was not the best time to get worked up like that over such issues. I was at a party and needed to relax and... enjoy myself. So I changed the direction of my thoughts and tried to admire the whole set up. The place looked a little mystical in the moonlight. The cool night breeze added to the charm.

It's funny how I always want to go to parties and invariably end up being alone in a corner somewhere. And it's even funnier how I always find a lonely corner in every party. It's true, what that crow taught us – where there is a will, there is a way.

I should have got a book or something along with me to this party. That definitely would have helped me kill time (in a productive way). Or maybe, I should try to socialize a little. How could it be that I was the only one who didn't like crowds and loud music at the party? There had to be more people of my kind. I looked at the distant hall beyond the garden, pulsating with dancing lights and music.

That was when I saw a girl coming out of the hall. Sometimes it's really cool, the way God is keenly listening to your thoughts and then gets playful, isn't it? A minute ago I was thinking that I should try and mingle and right then God sends a girl. But how should I approach her? Should I just walk up to her and say 'hi'? Or wait for her to go and sit somewhere and then try striking up a conversation? As I contemplated all this, I realized how desperate I would appear if I went ahead and did any of that. So I just chucked the whole idea and looked away.

The huge fountain caught my attention again. It was quite a piece of work I must say – so intricately made. There were life-size sculptures bearing a human form and water was flowing out from

God knows where all. And the sculptures looked quite real. I stood there in front of the fountain observing it closely. Suddenly I heard a voice say,

"Not a major party animal, are you?"

What? Was it a magical fountain? Did the sculptures talk?

"It's quite a marvel, isn't it?" the voice said again. And that was when I realized that the voice was not coming from any of the figures in the fountain, rather from somewhere behind me.

I turned around to see who it was and to my surprise, it was the girl whom I had seen coming out of the party hall. She was dripping wet, with sweat I assumed, and she was still panting from the heavy dancing she must have been doing inside the hall. She kind of looked my age (or I was just being plain optimistic).

"It sure is," I smiled.

Now before I go any further, I must inform you that I am no charmer. In fact, I am the clumsiest person one can possibly come across. If you looked at my face, you would think it's a tomato in disguise. And if you looked at the rest of me, you would wonder why someone would put a tomato at the end of a pencil and place it on a stand.

She smiled back, "So, having booze alone in the garden? Or do you have someone hiding in the bushes waiting for you?"

"No, no. Nothing like that," I said. What was wrong with her? Why would she think like that?

"Look at you! You are blushing," she said as she sat down on a bench.

"No, no!" I protested.

With her eyes fixed on me, and a smile of amusement, she said, "Come, sit here," as she patted the empty seat next to her.

I went and sat near her like a dog following an order. She did not look like someone I would want to offend.

One thing that I noticed beyond the moonlight, the fountain, the sculptures and the breeze, were the mosquitoes. And one mosquito bite was starting to itch real bad, on my elbow. And I could not resist scratching.

"One of the many problems with Gurgaon – mosquitoes. If you want, we can go in," she said.

How could I accept that? How could I *ever* take such a suggestion from this super attractive girl sitting next to me? She was saying that *mosquitoes* were bothering me? Now, I might not look all that macho, but I am not such a sissy either.

"No, no. Mosquitoes don't bother me," I flashed a smile back at her.

"You know something? You interest me," she said as she smiled at me.

I looked at her silently and smiled back. It was definitely a very weird day – she was finding me interesting – she wanted to talk to me!

"You must be wondering what kind of a strange girl I am, showing up like this talking to a total stranger," she said.

"No, that's not what I was thinking." I let out a little laugh and repeated, "That was really not what I was thinking."

"It's just that the guy who sits in a corner, alone at a party, not trying to peep into other girls' tops is generally a safe stranger to be with. And believe me, I know men. And you for sure are one of the innocent types."

Something within me made me take it as a compliment.

"Thank you," I said.

"You are welcome," she replied.

After a short stretch of silence, she asked, "You came alone to this party? No friends?"

"I came with friends. But they are all inside, drinking, dancing and… chasing girls."

"Ok," she smiled.

"What about you? How come you are alone?" I asked.

"Well, I came to this party coz of a friend who has this giant crush on a guy from her office, who was coming to this party. She *had* to meet him here and she had nobody to take along with her, so here I am. She is inside by the way, dancing with that guy," she winked.

"Ok." I smiled.

She kept looking at me for a while and then finally spoke up, "Show me your right hand." And she flicked her hair back with a quick movement of her head.

"You know palmistry?" I said as I wiped my palm against my jeans to wipe off the sweat.

"Not really, but I can read some stuff."

I stretched out my palm towards her.

"You know what they say about reading someone's palm after

sunset?" she said as she held my hand by the fingers and drew it under her eyes.

I felt a sudden urge to quickly withdraw my hand. Was she a witch? Was she gonna cast a spell on me in the middle of the night? Oh my God! She was gonna turn me into a stone sculpture! Oh my God!!! All these sculptures around me were living people once upon a time. And this woman here turned them all into stone. That is why the first thing she did was praise the sculptures when she started talking to me! No, no, no!

"Relax," she said, "It's not the one whose palm is being read who needs to worry, it's the one who is reading that needs to worry."

I looked at her confused.

"They say that if you read someone's palm after sunset, all his ill-deeds get transferred onto you."

"Oh no!"

"But looking at you," she said as she looked into my eyes, "I have a feeling, that I don't have much to worry about. You don't look like someone who has done many *bad* things."

Oh God! The mosquitoes here were really nasty or what? Now they were eating up my legs. It was strange how they managed to bite me right through my socks.

"Look, if I am troubling you, then I am sorry. I don't want to impose," she said, as she noticed that I was getting uncomfortable.

"No, no, nothing like that, it's not you who's bothering me. What do you read?" I asked.

"Well, apart from weak health, indecisiveness, and too much

unnecessary worrying... I don't see much."

"Ahmm."

"Were you a weak student?" she asked.

"No." The word instantly came out like a defensive reflex. What did she mean? I never failed in school, not even once. In fact, I was quite a topper.

"Ok, ok, sorry. In that case I can see a deviation in your career. You are not gonna pursue what you are professionally trained for."

Ok. Either she was good at what she was doing, or she already knew quite a bit about me.

"And," she said and suddenly fell silent as if she had seen something terribly drastic.

I looked at her, worried.

"You have blood on your hands."

"Oh, no, that's no blood. That must be ketchup," I said as I laughed in relief.

"No, I mean, like a murder. Your palm says that you will murder someone someday."

I looked back at her, petrified. What was she saying? That was just not possible. I never even killed an ant. Murdering a living person? That was beyond crazy.

Suddenly she broke into a fit of laughter and said,

"God, I was just joking, look at you!"

I gaped back at her shocked.

"What do you do by the way?" she said as she let go of my hand. "I mean, are you… still studying, or are you working?"

"I am an architect… working as an architect, I mean. But I don't enjoy my work much," I said, scratching my elbow. These mosquitoes! $^&#&*^&*

"And may I ask why you don't like practising architecture?"

"Hmm. Why don't I like practising architecture? That's because I just don't like working," I laughed.

She looked back at me with an awkward smile.

"No actually, ahum," I said, clearing my throat. "Why I don't like working *as an architect* is because most of the time when I am making those blueprints for those buildings… I just feel that… we don't need to construct all that. I mean, where I work, they specialize in luxury apartments. I don't know… it just does not feel right. The other day we were selecting tiles for this water feature and the client wanted these particular tiles that have gold foil laminated between glass sheets, that cost 22k per tile. Can you beat that! 22 *thousand* – that is the average salary of a fresh, young, qualified professional in a metropolitan city like ours for crying out loud!"

She looked at me and it seemed that she was thinking hard.

"And you know, that guy, he wants *gold leafing* done on the wooden panels flanking the sides of the corridor at the entrance."

She continued looking at me silently.

"What do you do?" I asked as I looked at her and tried to figure out what a girl who looked like that must do for a living.

"I am a journalist," she said, smiling smartly.

What? She was a journalist? She looked more like a model. Maybe she was a fashion journalist.

"Like a fashion journalist?" I asked.

"I work for *The Indian* and as sad as it might be, they don't have a fashion segment."

Alright, she looked nothing like a hard core, serious journalist. She did not even come close to the way Barkha Dutt looked.

"...you know about the paper, right? *The Indian*?"

"Yes, yes. I do. I mean, who doesn't? And it's really great to meet you. I have always wanted to do something for the... society, for ... a better cause. Being in touch with you would really be helpful I feel."

"Sure thing," she smiled back.

And that was the time we exchanged our email ids.

It was a great party, a wonderful evening and the weather was excellent. But the mosquitoes were really spoiling it all. I mean not a single minute had passed without my having to scratch a stupid, irritating mosquito bite.

"The mosquitoes are really troubling you, aren't they?" she asked.

"I can't deny that, I guess."

"You know, technically, the mosquitoes should be aiming for me more, as I am sweating, and hence emitting more body odour."

What? Mosquitoes are attracted by your body odour?!

"You know mosquitoes are attracted to you by your body odour, right?"

"Oh yes, yes, completely. That is not a new piece of information at all," I instantly replied.

She looked back at me smiling. I was sure she was smiling because she was happy to know that I already knew that. She didn't think that I didn't know.

"Can we go in? I am a little hungry. Is this what happens when mosquitoes suck too much blood out of you? These... tiny... flying vampires!" I said.

"Well, that I don't know. Maybe the mosquitoes around here would know better. Maybe you can try talking to them some time. As for being hungry, I can definitely have a snack."

Today when I look back, that very evening marked my 'pack up' from this city.

The boy who lived

After his annoying remark, I gave Abhinav a look that has actually shut him up. We have been travelling in silence after he took a newspaper out of his bag and began reading it.

I rest my head on the headrest of the tall chair and close my eyes, trying to relax.

"The dengue, it's quite an outbreak this year. They are saying the figures are the highest this time," he says after a while.

"Yes, that's true. Who would know that better than I do?" I say, as my thoughts catapult back in time again.

Exactly 15 days later, (after the party where I met that 'mystery girl') I found myself being dragged on a stretcher in the corridors of a hospital. (Now I am not gonna name the hospital here, as that would be like promoting the hospital. I do acknowledge that the people there actually saved my life but... you never know how they may take my words and might just... sue me.) The doctor's tip was not working. Each time the temperature shot up beyond 104°C, the cold shower was not bringing the temperature down... How would it when I didn't follow it in the first place! (What? A cold shower in the month of January, do you think that is easy to follow?) So I set out to go to the hospital and see the doctor, the bumpy cycle rickshaw ride drained whatever little energy I had left. And when the doctor was running along by my side as I was being pushed on a stretcher, I could not resist asking her,

"Doctor, am I gonna live?"

The doctor looked at me, smiled and said, "Yes." She was quite an elegant woman. These big, glossy hospitals take the best looking doctors I tell you, *Grey's Anatomy* is not all that far from reality.

I am not gonna get into the details... like how they took me to the ward and did a basic check up and I had to take my shirt off and realized how terribly... smelly I was at that time, and I apologized to the doctor for not maintaining the best hygiene. To which she smiled pleasantly again and said, "It's ok." Or that later I had to take so many liquids and IV fluids that I became a constant peeing machine. All I am gonna tell you is that my platelet count dropped so disastrously that the doctors also freaked out at one point of time and I was asked to inform my parents and ask them to come over from my hometown. So my Mom came running and screaming and shook up the whole hospital and threatened all the doctors that she would kill everyone in that hospital if anything happened to me. But such a situation never arose. Soon my condition took a miraculous turn and I lived! *I am the boy who lived!!!*

My Mom, ladies and gentlemen

"Which station have we reached?" Abhinav asks. For various reasons, I am not enjoying talking to him and he can't keep quiet even for five minutes.

"I don't know," I say. I am least interested in knowing what station we have reached. Unless it is Ambala and Abhinav has to get off here.

He looks at me all dewy-eyed and says, "It's a really great feeling to come back and visit your hometown, isn't it, the place where you grew up, where you were born."

"It sure is," I sigh, reminiscing about the last few days.

"You are not staying here, we are taking you back," my mother declared with complete authority. I had been discharged from the hospital and we were back to my two-bedroom apartment – Mom and me.

"But Mom! I have… a life here. My work… my job…" Actually

that was not why I was upset and why I did not want to go back. What I was *actually* thinking was – 'What? What about my friends and my... life! The movies, the restaurants, the coffee shops!!!'

"No way," she continued, "Can you see that packet lying there?" she said, pointing at a plastic bag lying in a corner of my room. "Do you know what that is?"

"Mangoes," I uttered meekly.

"Yes, those are the mangoes I sent you last *August* that the tree at our house bore *last summer*. And you have not even opened it. God! I don't even want to think what has become of those mangoes. It's almost February for heaven's sake!"

Actually that is not true. I did open the packet. Even had a few. But then one day I noticed too many ants in the room and in order to protect the mangoes from the ants, I packed them up again and put them in a bucket of water. And it was after about a month or so that I found that the ants were gone, and felt that the packet would be safe out of the water. But I never got around to opening it again and eating the mangoes. I work late nights you know. And if work gets done early, there is always some movie or the other to catch. And at times friends call to meet up. So I generally eat out. There is hardly any time to take care of all this.

"I know why you didn't eat those mangoes. You eat outside food all the time. The doctor was telling me that your immunity levels are very low. And one of the reasons for that is that you are eating all the food that you should not be eating."

"That... is not true." I said, hesitantly.

"Don't you lie to me!" she thundered back. And after a short pause she said, "I hope you realize you are lucky to be alive. Not everyone is fortunate enough to recover from a case of malaria coupled with dengue *and* jaundice. Do you know how many people have *died* of such cases in *that very* hospital?"

"I am not lying. I don't have outside food… all the time. Only sometimes do I eat out…" Ok, there is no point in arguing.

"And I don't know why you eat that food that they serve in the train when so many times I have told you not to."

Oh my God! How does she know this? I must deny, I must deny this right now! There is no way she can find out. There are no hidden cameras in the train, *I know that*.

"Mom, I never eat train food."

"Don't you lie to me!"

"I am *not lying*."

"What is that?" she said, pointing to my rucksack lying in another corner.

"My… bag?" I said meekly. Oh Damn! Oh damn! I had no idea this was coming.

"And what is there in its front pocket?"

The food that she packed for me for the train journey, which was like a month and a half ago.

"I don't know… some stuff maybe… a book or something I must have read during the journey…" I stammered.

"It has the food that I packed for you for your last train journey. You didn't even open it. And you don't even unpack your bags? The food has got all kinds of moulds and fungus coating it by now. I almost puked at the mere sight of it. No wonder your apartment stinks like crazy."

Ok, but I can explain. The maid back there at our house, she cooks the most terrible food. It's worse than plain boiled vegetables. No normal human being can have that. And besides, train food may be very unhygienic, but it smells really good and is completely irresistible, even more so when you are hungry and have not eaten for hours. And someone really needs to be crazy not to have those ice creams they serve at the end of the meal. They had just had a tie-up with Barista you know.

"And look at all that? How do you figure out which clothes are clean and which ones are dirty?" she asked, pointing at the heaps of clothes distributed all over the apartment.

"And I don't even want to get started about all the garbage and the rotten fruits and vegetables lying in the kitchen," she continued.

"*Mom*, I told you. I have a very busy life here. I don't have time —"

"But you have all the time for this."

Oh my God! She has discovered my *movie ticket collection*!! May Day! May Day!

"I counted them. There are a total of 564."* She said this looking straight into my eyes.

Ok, how do I cover up on this one? *How do I cover up on this one*?!!!

"And most of them are night shows. How many times have I told you not to go to night shows? You know the crime rate around here. You are not a kid anymore."

---

* In my defense, it took me *three years* to watch that many movies. The text on most of them is vanishing. Maybe I should get them laminated or something to preserve them.

Uh! She was right. (And obviously there was no point in fighting it anymore.) I was not a child anymore. And clearly, I was not able to manage on my own here.

Pack-up

"Quite some luggage you have with you," Abhinav says. I should really give it up – the hope that he is ever gonna shut up.

"Ya, I do actually," I say.

"I think they are a total of eight bags," he says.

"Bang on," I say with a smile of irritation as I see a twinkle of useless achievement in his eyes.

"Are you going back forever?" he asks.

"No, only for a few months," I reply matter-of-factly.

And that is the truth. I am gonna come back after I regain my health. My health has hit rock bottom and I need some time to regain my strength. This is the only reason why I am going back.

Abhinav goes back to reading his paper. I look up at the luggage rack and see the eight bags neatly stacked on it. I can't help remembering the time when we were packing all my stuff.

"Rishabh, are you done with your packing? Your books and drawings are still all over the place!" my Mom called from the other room. It's like this huge celebration for her – getting all my stuff and my moving back home. She has been generously giving out a tip of not less than 50 rupees to each and every helper who is helping us pack; even if he moves a box by just an inch, she gives him the money. But that is how she is, always up and about and cheerful.

It was final that I was going back. Everything was set, but one thing still remained to be dealt with – the office. I was yet to inform them that I was leaving and was not sure as to when I would be back. So the very next day, there I was – in front of my boss, sitting on a chair across the table.

"What do you mean you are leaving? We need you here Rishabh," my boss said, looking shocked.

I smiled back.

"We have a wonderful project lined up for you. We were gonna hand you the new project we got the other day – a luxury holiday home for Zazzy E, the great Punjabi pop sensation, as they call him," he said, as he rolled his eyes, smiling cheerfully.

"It's near Shimla. No, no. We won't let you go; you are a part of us *Rishabh*," he continued.

I knew what he meant. What he was actually saying was – 'My dear employee, if you plan to quit your job without prior notice, you need to produce documental evidence, proof.'* Oh I knew him inside out. And I had come prepared.

"I can't help it ma'am," I said, plastering a smile on my face. "The doctors have advised me to be under observation for a while. They say that a relapse would be fatal," I said as I took the letter my doctor had written and signed, and placed it on the table.

---

* These corporates, I hate the way they work. It's so... robotic and... un-human.

"*Ooh!* That is so *sad*," he said as he unfolded it and began reading it.

"I know. It's not easy for me either." I smiled. I hated it when I had to stoop to their level in order to deal with them.

"I guess there is nothing we can do then," he said, smiling after going through the letter.

"I guess so."

More smiles and silence.

"I guess I'll just go and... clear up my desk," I said.

"Yaa. I think you should *do* that," he said as he lowered his eyes again to the drawing that he was working on.

"All right then," I said and left his cabin. He didn't look up or say bye or anything. Now that I was officially out of the office, he didn't need to be nice to me. (Or even talk to me or acknowledge my existence.)

After that I went and emptied my desk.

So you see, I was not fired – I quit.

Oh, how much I love her

The train is quite peaceful right now. Almost everyone is sleeping. I take the earphones out of the bag and plug the jack into the phone socket. I love listening to music while travelling by train – I find it really relaxing. I am about to plug the earphones in my ears when (nosy) Abhinav butts in again.

"Are you going home for matrimonial purposes?" he asks.

Some people just can't mind their own business, can they? I simply smile back at him and say,

"No." I don't want him to ask me more about it. I have no matrimony plans as of now. And frankly if you ask me, I don't have much of a say in it either – it's all up to Superna. Who is Superna? Well, she is my girlfriend. (Hah! I do have a girlfriend, what did you think?) And we have not broken up; we are just going through a rough patch. Ok, I'll tell you what exactly happened.

We have been in love for three years now. Last year she went to London for a one-year Masters' programme in business and since then things have not been great between us. Initially it was 'I am busy, can we talk later?' on the phone. Then it was 'I am in a class, I will call you later' and then it was simply not attending my calls. I have been sending her gifts and presents all the way across the seas and all she does is send me a *thank you* mail. But things were more or less fine till like three months back. Till that dreadful day when she called me. I was so happy to see her number flash on the cell phone screen. I greeted the call with a huge smile.

"Hi! How *are* you? Long time!" I said.

"Ya," she said.

"So, how are you? How is everything? I missed you so much." I don't know how many of you would understand that when you love someone, you really don't know why you love her so much. But that thought keeps hovering inside your mind to bring a smile to your face, and you just want to sit by her side and hold her hand.

"I am good," she said, sounding a little hesitant.

"Rishabh, I just wanted to say that... I think that things are not working out between us. I am here and... I have a completely new circle and I don't know when, or if at all, I am gonna come back."

"What do you mean you don't know when you're gonna come back? You said you were coming in October!"

"Yes, I am gonna come then, but only for a few weeks."

"Superna, are you breaking up with me?" I freaked out.

"... I just feel that we should take things a little slow or... maybe take a break for a while."

Ok, so I won't go into all the details of how I meekly hung up after that. Cried to myself, sitting alone in the room. And then sent one mail to Superna every day for a full two weeks saying the same thing over and over again, that I loved her and I was sorry if I had ever hurt her and I just wanted her to give me one more chance and I wanted things to be the way they were earlier and she just sent back a few mails saying that our relationship was over. But believe you me – this is not how our relationship is gonna end. I know I am gonna get back with her.

Please don't embarrass me!

Thank God we have crossed Ambala. Abhinav is off the train. This train journey feels quite nice now and I am actually enjoying it. After almost a decade, here I am shifting back to my hometown.

If you book your tickets in a good AC compartment, the experience is not all that bad these days. Apart from an occasional tiny little cockroach or a rat, you don't really see anything too disturbing. I am telling you, the standards are really improving. And look at the surroundings – everything is clean. And the tube lights inside those luminars are working; no lizards trapped inside them whatsoever. These rugged velvet seat covers look nice and clean. The paint all around looks clean. No window glass has any crack in it. Everything looks nice and light blue and... fresh. I am telling you; it was not because of the food they serve in the train that I had that bout of food poisoning earlier.* I turn around and look at Mom sitting beside me. She is up now and looking completely psyched out. She has her chiffon *dupatta* wrapped all around her face in such a way that she can easily be mistaken for an Afghani immigrant.

"Mom... what is all this?" I ask, resisting the urge to pull off that cover from her face.

"You have no idea how many germs are floating around us right now. The AC compartments are a hazard. You should also cover your face like this. I have a spare *dupatta*. But you are not gonna listen. Thank God! At least this time you will be home if you fall sick. And I can make sure things don't get as bad as they did the last time." She stares at me as she says that. And after a small pause, she says, "and you remember the *three fold path of precaution* the doctor asked you to follow, don't you?"

"Yes Mom, I remember."

"Ok, tell me then, what is it?" she says.

---

* Which led to a two-day hospital stay.

All right, now this is embarrassing. I know for a fact that the bunch of kids (who are most probably college students) sitting behind us are paying more attention to us than they should be. They are leaning forward and listening to our conversation like nobody's business.

"Come on. I am waiting."

She won't give it up. I know. The only way to end this is to surrender.

"(1)   Take Vitamin C tablets daily for three months – it's my life line.

(2)   Do not let mosquitoes come anywhere near me. Use Odomos – it's my weapon, my armour.

(3)   Wipe my hands with a sanitizer each time I come back from a crowded place or am about to eat something."

I swear I can almost hear those kids at the back laughing. It's really dumb you know. I am sure they are sitting there and calling me a complete freak. When they have no idea what I have been through. *I almost died you know*! And even the doctors acknowledge that. My doctor, when she was telling me the T.F.P.P.,* she was so serious that I felt her eyes were gonna pop out any second then. But anyway, what did I care about a couple of bored college kids? They were just looking for entertainment.

"Hey *Bhagwaan*! Did you put on Odomos before getting on the train?" Mom flips again.

"Yes Mom, and so much that even the last mosquito in the last coach at the end of the train is hiding somewhere traumatized."

---

* T.F.P.P. = Three Fold Path of Precaution.

"Show me," she demanded. Oh my God! It was time for the test. I could so feel the kids peeking at me through the tiny gap between the seats.

I held out my arm for Mom to see. She first rubbed it to see if it was greasy enough after the application and then smelt it.

"Ok."

I give her a 'please-get-a-hold-of-yourself' look.

"What?" she says defensively. "Someone has to take care of all this. If you completely decide not to."

My mother. She really freaks out, doesn't she? And I can understand her concern. She just doesn't want me to fall prey again to all the things I had just recovered from. They say that the malarial parasite (the one I had) is not that easy to kill. And even if a single parasite is left alive inside you, there are chances of a relapse. She just cares for me too much to behave normally. I can't help smiling, looking at her.

I lean back in my seat and look outside. It's a nice sunny day. I look at the clear sky through the tinted glass of the window, and the expansive golden fields rushing past me, remembering how they ran past in the opposite direction, eight years ago, when I was going to join college and start a new life – a new life in a big city. And God! It was great. I won't think twice before saying that it was the best time of my life. But I guess nothing lasts forever. Everything has... a life. And when I really think about it, I'm sure I will enjoy going back to my hometown. (Abhinav did have a point there.) That small little town, where everyone knows everyone. Where there is peace and quiet everywhere. I wouldn't have to keep running all day because I was getting late for office, which was a half hour drive from my place or... because I had to be at a meeting at 11 'by all means' and there was no way I could make it on time. So what if my friends weren't around? All of us have the phone and the Internet these days. It's so not difficult to stay in touch any more. Ok, now I just can't wait to be home. Peace and quiet, here I come!

Who's that dog?

Oh Gruntas! What the hell is that noise?! It's 6 o'clock in the morning and I am sure it's a baby that I hear screaming and yelling. I force open my eyes and have to squint for a good 15 seconds or so before my eyes acclimatize to the light after absolute darkness. I step outside my room and follow the sound to the balcony. I can still hear a sharp screeching sound, but I see nothing. Maybe it's a daily phenomenon or something here. Maybe it happens like everyday here – invisible babies yelling and screaming every morning. I should check with Mom.

I go to Mom's room and knock on the door.

"Wait a minute," Mom replies half asleep.

"What is it?" she looks at me with eyes wide open, looking dazed as she opens the door in a while.

"What's this sound?" I ask.

"What sound?" she asks.

The shrieks are still very much on.

"That!" I say. It was so prominent, how could anyone miss it?

"Oh that. It sounds like a puppy. Must be outside somewhere in the street." She is not bothered.

What! There is a helpless puppy outside in the street all by itself! I must do something!!

"Now go back to sleep," she says as she turns around and walks away.

"Yes." I must not let her know that I am going to look for the puppy. She would never let me go.

"And don't go chasing that puppy. These things are nothing more than a bundle of germs," she says as climbs onto the bed.

* * *

It's been over three minutes, I have been looking for the puppy but it's nowhere to be found. I have searched behind almost every bush.

But there is no way I can give up this search – the poor thing is in pain!

"Rishabh! What are you doing there?" Mom shouts from the balcony.

Oh my God!!! It's Mom! I must quit the search right now and go back!!!

"I… was just… going for a… jog. Yes." That is believable; moreover, she would be happy to know that. Jogging is good for health.

"I want you back in the house *right now*. Do you know how many mosquitoes are there in those bushes? Do you know how *dangerous* it is for you?"

All right, now she is talking pretty loudly, and I am sure that everyone in the whole colony has his/her ear pressed against the windows listening to all this and is giggling away to glory. That is how things are in a small town. And I am 25, for crying out loud, why is she treating me like a 3 year old? Fine, I agree that I behave like a kid at times, but that doesn't alter my age. I seriously don't understand why she treats me this way. And I have my reasons to behave kiddishly. It's very important not to let the kid inside you die, ever. It's the only way to keep your life beautiful.

"Ok, *fine*! You *never* let me do anything," I say as I walk back to the gate, my shoulders hunched in disappointment.

Just then the howling of the puppy becomes even louder and sharper. And then suddenly it starts barking. I cannot help it, I have to turn back and see.

It's a tiny, brown puppy! And he is limping and coming out of a bush onto the street. And he is coming to me! I run to him. Poor little thing, he had been hiding in the bush wanting me to find him! Poor puppy! I pick him up and hug him. Dogs are God's best creation I tell you.

"Rishabh put that dog down right now!" my Mom shouts.

* * *

The puppy has a fractured leg. And there was no way I could have left him on the street out there to die. With one leg injured and the others so tiny too, he would never have survived. He was sure to be run over by a car or something. But Mom is furious. She has decided not to talk to me as long as I don't give up the puppy. But anyway, he's been in our house for over nine hours now and Mom has not taken any drastic steps. So this kind of means that he is staying. I am in the lawn right now, washing the puppy.

Mom is in the kitchen.

After pacing to and fro in the kitchen for over five minutes, she finally comes out and yells, "The puppy cannot stay in this house."

"Calm down Mom, it's just a puppy, not a... rattle snake!" I say.

"It's a stray puppy! It's gonna litter our whole house –"

"It's just a little baby, he's not gonna do anything."

She stands there staring at me as I continue washing the puppy. I am being very careful with him, trying my best not to touch the leg that is hurt. But still the puppy occasionally howls. And when he is not howling, he looks straight into my eyes with his soft, adoring... loving eyes. There is something completely divine about dogs and puppies I tell you. Just look at this lovely little thing – light brown fur, tiny little white spot on his chest and his paws look as if they have been dipped in white paint.

Mom storms back inside and I let out a sigh of relief.

Actually, I'll tell you the reason why I got this puppy home. Not that the puppy is *not* completely adorable or anything, it so is – I have already fallen in love with him. But there is another reason – back when I was a kid, I saw this movie – *The Breakfast Club*. And in that movie there was this scene, where that girl with dark hair (and black clothes) said as her hair fell all across her face, *'when you grow up, your heart dies.'* That particular line, for some reason, left a very deep impression on me. And as a result, till date, if I feel like doing anything, and if I feel the slightest tug of... practicality or *maturity* telling me not to do it, I simply go right ahead and just do it, because I do not want my heart to die. I believe that it's the *maturity* that actually kills our heart as we grow up.

Completely lost in my thoughts, I start patting the puppy looking at him with unseeing eyes. My Mom comes out of the house again, stands in front of me with her hands on her hips, and says, "The puppy must go out this evening."

Ok, this is a good sign. She is not picking up the puppy and throwing it out. This means that she is indirectly giving her approval for the puppy to stay.

"And we need to go to a wedding today evening. Make sure you don't make any plans and are ready on time."

"Mom! You know how much I hate weddings."

She is walking away when she hears me and turns around again.

"You must go to this wedding and build your contacts if you want to stay in this town and work," she says as she glares at me.

"But... I am not sure... how long I will be staying here," I stammer.

"It's ok, we are not sure of many things at times. But that does not mean that we stop taking actions and stop planning."

Weddings are painful affairs

Did I ever mention how much I hate weddings? Not only because they play like the most distasteful music most unbelievably loudly and that makes you completely deaf (no, that's not the reason, I have been to many New Year parties at various local clubs – I can handle that). But also because everyone who comes and talks to you is not just talking to you, he (or she) is actually *judging you*. Like if an aunty comes and asks you, 'How are you Beta?' what she actually means is 'How are you now? Last time you looked terrible.' Or if she asks, 'How's work going?' she actually means, 'How are things at work? I heard that everyone in your office got a raise but you.' And not only all this, just look at everything around – the decorations are a riot – no colour scheme or style whatsoever. And all the uncles with their thick beards dancing away. Look at that one for instance, dancing with a glass of whisky in one hand and a lady's hand in the other. Thinking in his drunkenness that she is his wife (or may be fully aware that she is not!), when she is actually his neighbour.

"Hello Beta." I hear someone call me. Ok, must activate my defense systems – it's Cheema Aunty – the fat taunting aunty from the house next door. She and Mom are co-kitty members. She is very nice and full of smiles when she talks to you but her words actually feel like spurs on your skin.

"How are you?"

Oh no! Not that question again.

"I am good Aunty, how are you?"

"Never been better Beta," she says with a smile as she winks at me.

"So, how come you are in town?" she asks.

Red alert! RED ALERT!

"Have not been keeping well lately, Aunty. So thought of spending some time at home." I smile back.

"Oh! God *bless* you. You were in Gurgaon, right?"

"Yes," I say as I take a sip from the glass of orange juice in my hand.

"And you had a job there, right?"

"Amhumm..." I nod.

"Have you given up the job?" she enquires as her wicked smile returns to her face.

"Yes, I had to quit. I was not sure when I would go back so..." I trail off into silence. I can just sense she is gonna pass a mean comment now.

"Hmm, the recession is also on these days. Those companies can't afford things as they could have before. It's a very sad affair."

See? You can't blame me for not liking this lady. She is actually saying it right to my face that I am lying and I never fell sick, that instead I am trying to cover up and make a story.

"How much were you getting there *vasay*?" she asks.

Ok, does she even realize that it's not very polite to ask this?

"Something like 40."

"Hmm, it doesn't make any sense to leave a job and come to this town, if you ask *me*."

Does it make any sense to give your advice to someone when it's completely unasked for? I don't say anything. I just simply look back at her and smile.

"You are an architect, right?" she asks.

"Yes."

"You know your uncle?... My husband, I mean. He can help you get projects. He used to work for the municipal department, or whatever it's called. You should come over to our house sometime. He didn't come to this wedding, otherwise you could have met him here only."

Thank God for that!

"But that's for later. I also have a project for you."

"Really?" I force a smile.

"Yes, we are planning to build another storey for our house. And you can design that."

"Sure." I smile.

Help! HELP!!!

"So, when are you getting married?"

Ok, here is the other thing, the minute you turn 25, everyone around you just screams and jumps at you and starts to poke you and ask you the same question over and over again – 'When are you getting married? When are you getting married?'

"Oh come on. It can't be that you don't have a girlfriend. Why don't you tell us about her and we can start arranging the wedding. It's *not* good to be in love with someone and wait so long without getting married you know."

That may be true. But what if the person you love does not feel the same way about you? In that case, forcibly marrying someone would definitely not make things any better. This aunty is a complete dumbhead I tell you. She does not know *anything*.

"Anyway, I need to go and catch up with my other friends," she says as she winks at me again. "I'll see you around. And do come to our house. I will be waiting." She winks again. Ok, seriously, What's wrong with her eye? She needs to see an eye doctor.

The fat aunty leaves and I turn around to see my Mom almost rushing to me.

"What was Mrs. Cheema saying?" she asks, bursting with curiosity.

"Nothing, she was just saying that she is planning to construct another –"

"Yes! My plan worked."

I don't like fat aunties

Ok, going to the wedding was a really bad idea. Not only that I am still irritated about the fact that I was totally humiliated by F.C.A.* But also because I can't get my mind off Superna now.

I need to talk to someone about it. What's the time? I look at my

---

* F.C.A. = Fat Cheema Aunty

watch and it's 11 o'clock. Great! Natasha must be online. I will simply pour out all my anxiety on chat... remember Natasha, right? The girl from the party? I never told you her name, did I?

I log in to Gtalk and there she is, with her cute little display pic in which she is wearing blue eye lenses and looking completely ravishing in that aqua dress.

Rishabh – hi!

Natasha – hi! how are u?

Rishabh – i am god. how are u?

Rishabh – good*

Natasha – LOL i am also god!

Rishabh – ☺

Natasha – so, tell me, how have u been? how's ur home town treating you.

Rishabh – ummm, it's been ok.

Natasha – hmm, what's wrong?

Rishabh – i don't like the aunties here.

Natasha – OMG! u are being fixed up with an aunty to get married!!! u r doomed rishabh, u r doomed.

Rishabh – ☺ yes, very funny. no, there is nothing like that. it's just that... i don't like them.

Natasha – ok, and why do u have to like them?

Rishabh – because they are all around.

Natasha – does that mean that u also need to be around them?

Rishabh – hmm. aren't u gonna ask me what happened? and why do i not like fat aunties here?

Natasha – clearly some 'fat' aunty must have said something to u, and u are over reacting. i don't need to ask u. i know u well enough.

Rishabh – hmm. what should i do?

Natasha – meet old friends.

Rishabh – i don't have any friends here.

Natasha – it's your hometown, u must have some old school friends who are still there, right?

Rishabh – hmm yes. i do.

Natasha – so meet them. get pally with them, socialize with them, create your circle. expand your horizons rishabh!

Rishabh – ya, u r right.

Natasha – how's the puppy doing by the way?

Rishabh – oh, he is doing great. we have become great friends. he can't stay away from me for even a minute. he sleeps in my room. he has selected a corner, next to my old almirah which has all my precious belongings, saved up from childhood. he likes to cuddle next to it and sleep. maybe he finds the warmth of the memories from the cupboard comforting.

Natasha – that is nice to know ☺ now if you don't mind, i gtg. need to finish a story before I go to sleep tonight.

Rishabh – great! i mean no problem. what's it about?

Natasha – child labour, child abuse and children's right to education.

Rishabh – great! good luck with that. c u bye.

Natasha – cu bye.

→ **Natasha has signed out.**

Is that a great idea or what? I should completely do that – meet my old friends whom I went to school with! The ones I *grew up* with! I instantly log on to Facebook and go through my Friends list and visit the profiles of all the people who were my friends in school.

Ok, this looks good. There are a total of six friends who are still in this town. But I haven't been in touch with them for ages. Not that it would be odd when I met them or that I would not be able to strike up a conversation when I met them – I am completely capable of doing that. I grew up with them for heaven's sake! It's just that I don't have their contact number. And leaving a message here on Facebook does not seem to be the best idea. Most of them have not logged on for almost a year it seems. *But*, there is always a solution to everything. All the stuff that I have saved up from my school days is gonna come in handy today. All the books, notebooks, scrapbooks *and* phone books are gonna save the day.*

---

* I have had the most royal quarrels with my Mom about this old stuff and she has always threatened me that she would throw it all away one day when I am sleeping. But each time she says that, I roar so loudly that she has never been able to do that. Unlike me, she does not know, that these things are life saviors on days like today. It's impossible to stay alive without these things.

I dash to the old closet in my room and locate my own handmade, personalized Dennis the Menace phone book. The puppy is sleeping right next to it and I must not wake him up. Cos if I do, he is surely not gonna go off to sleep again and will look at me with those anticipating eyes expecting me to play with him.

I find my phone book and it is exactly as it was 10 years ago. Just that the edges are a bit worn and the spiral binding has snapped right in the middle. But it is completely usable and intact in most ways.

I pull it out softly and leaf through it. There are no cell numbers in the book. Obviously – we didn't have cell phones when I was in school. These are all landline numbers. I quickly jot down all the numbers I need and put the phone book back. It's too late in the night to call anyone right away, it's past 10. If I do, they are completely gonna take me for a maniac who calls them up in the middle of the night *after 10 years*. I'll call them up tomorrow morning. Maybe around 11 or something. That's a good time. Must go to sleep now. As it is the wedding has drained me of all my energy.

Please come back!

I just can't get myself to sleep. I have been trying to sleep for over an hour now but have only been staring at the ceiling like an owl. I hate that F.C.A.! Why did I ever go to that wedding! That stupid aunty has reminded me of Superna and now I just can't get my mind off her. What did Superna find wrong in me? If she came back, I would make every possible effort to keep her happy.

If she wanted expensive gifts, I would get them for her. I would...
treat her like a princess. For I always want to see her happy and
smiling. Maybe she has forgotten the way I feel about her. Maybe
I just need to remind her. YES! That is what I need to do. I
instantly fling the bedsheet off me and jump to my computer
table and turn it on, log in to my Gmail account and start typing a
mail,

Dear Superna,

I was lying in my bed, trying to sleep. But I just could not get your
sweet, lovely, beautiful, angel face off my mind. We were so good
together. We were so happy. Just give me one more chance. I
would do anything to make you happy. You know how much I
have always loved you. And just to let you know, I love you even
more now. It's true what they say – distance makes you grow
fodder. Please come back into my life. I can't live without you.

And no matter what happens, I will always love you.

Yours, today and forever,

Rishabh

I really hope she replies this time. She has not replied to my last
three mails. Anyway, I feel very relieved now. I can sleep. Good
that I sent her the mail. It's very important to express your love I
believe.

I turn off the computer and it makes that signature logging off
sound. As soon as the computer shuts down, I hear a moan. It's
the puppy, he is up. He gives me this lazy look and comes and lies
down next to my feet, cuddling against them.

He sleeps so peacefully. There is infinite innocence in his face. I
want to keep looking at him. I want to hold him in my lap and sit
like that forever. But it's really late and I must go sleep. I get up

and move my feet away from him and he starts to moan again. The puppy wants to be loved. The puppy wants someone to hold him as he sleeps. Had it been any other time, I would have ignored his need and walked away. But right now I can't do this to him – I know what it feels like not to be loved. I pick him up very gently and lay him on my bed. I start patting him and within seconds he falls asleep again with the same peaceful, innocent expression on his face as before.

* * *

Why would the bedsheet keep slipping off me? This is really irritating. I have pulled it back over myself I don't know how many times. It's really early in the morning and I just do not want to get up. And why should I get up? I have no reason whatsoever to get up this early.

I try pulling the sheet back over me to find it stuck somewhere.

I open my eyes and squint to see where it is stuck. The puppy has caught the corner of the sheet in his teeth and is jumping excitedly. As soon as he notices me moving, he starts barking.

But I still do not want to get up. I just cover my head with the bed sheet and snuggle up with my pillow.

"Rishabh! Get up!" There is some very loud knocking on the door. It's Mom.

"What is it?" I ask irritably.

"Either you turn this puppy out this instant or I will turn it out of the house," she sounds really angry. I can't really blame her – the sharp barking of the puppy is quite annoying.

"It's ok, I've got it," I reply as I stumble off my bed and fumble for my slippers, slip them on, pick up the puppy and open the door.

"If you take up something, you must take it up with full responsibility." She glares at me.

"Uh! I know. And please don't start all this so early in the morning."

I take the puppy out into the street so that he can do his business but the puppy just stands there and does nothing. What does he want then? Why was he being so impatient? When I take him back to the house he goes limping to the garden, stops bang in the centre and starts to howl. Ok, if it isn't that, then he must be hungry. I go to the kitchen and start looking for things I can feed him.

I pour milk into a bowl and put some crumbs of bread in it. It's quite a pleasant morning, soft rays of the morning sun touching the kitchen floor. The morning always brings with it such a fresh and pleasant feel isn't it? It's really beautiful if you notice it. I look outside the window and see the tree leaves swaying in the gentle breeze. My eyes fall on the little puppy in the lawn again, who has stopped howling and is staring intently at the door through which I had entered the house. It's really amazing isn't it? I mean, this small little baby is in a completely alien place, badly hurt. When I look into his eyes, I see such trust. And the poor thing has a fractured leg. And he is not on any medication, yet he keeps moving around. Very strong and... courageous of him I must say. I can't even imagine myself matching up to all this if I ever get stuck in such a situation.

I have read *Marley and Me* and I know that animals can teach you a lot. Marley is such a nice name. I should name the puppy Marley too. But that's not original. I want him to have an original, unique name. Ok, so as he is a small puppy, we can call him Chota Kutta. And as he is very strong and courageous, you know, keeps limping all over the house even with a broken leg and... howls and cries only when he is... hungry, his middle name can be Gabru*. And since he is young, his last name can be... Young. So his full name becomes Chotta Kutta Gabru Young. I think it's a terrific name. I hear Mom say, in an irritated tone, as she enters the kitchen,

"Young puppies are very restless and impatient."

"Yes, and I am feeding him," I say as I pick up the bowl and move out.

To my utmost terror, the puppy is not there.

"Hey... Puppy!" I call out. No response, no puppy appears.

I whistle and call out "Puppy" again. Still nothing.

For the next 50 minutes I frantically search the whole house. But Chotta Kutta Gabru Young is nowhere to be found. Feeling exhausted more than I ever remember feeling, I step into the house. Mom is still in the kitchen.

"Gabru Chotta Kutta Jawan is gone!" I say in desperation.

"That's how street puppies are. They have such habits. I tried to explain, but you never listen," she says as she carries on with her work.

After a second or two, she looks at me and says, "He might come back, you know."

---

* For those who do not know, Gabru is a Punjabi word that means 'a young, handsome boy or man, full of youth'.

"I don't know." I sigh as I get up and walk to my room. I have seen it happen in the movies; lost puppies find their way back home after their big adventures and everything becomes as good as it was earlier. But this is real life. And no such thing is gonna happen here. For some unknown reason I am convinced that Gabru Jawan is never gonna find his way back home and is gonna be lost in the streets where I would never ever go myself. But there is nothing I can do about it. It's just something I will have to live with for the rest for my life.

I drag myself to my room and slump on the bed wondering how depressing things could get. There was just this one thing that was pulling me through these terrible times and now even that was gone. This is it – this is how the rest of my life is gonna be – lying on my bed in my empty room, with this… dull paint on the walls and this… dull bedspread, and this dull computer and… Hey! I should check my mail! Superna might have replied! Yes! I should totally do that!!! I immediately hop onto my computer chair and switch on my computer. And it takes me two minutes to find out that my love, Superna, has not replied. Hmm, she must have been busy. It's ok, it's not that she is not replying because she thinks I am a maniac or something. She is just stuck with work.

I scroll down my Friends list to see who all are online and just then an email pops up.

✉ You have 1 new message

It's Superna! It's her mail! She replied! Ok, this is the best day of my life.

I start reading the mail right away.

Rishabh,

This has gone way beyond the line now. You are behaving like a complete maniac. We both know that we tried our best and things did not work out. You had been irritating me since like... forever now and I didn't want to be rude to you and that is why I didn't reply to your previous mails. But you have left me with no choice. It's high time that you move on with your life, and let me move on with mine. I don't know much about relationships, but I know one thing for sure – if we stay together, neither of us would be happy. And you know we have tried that.

And stop freaking out; there are a lot of girls out there. And one of them *is* gonna end up happily with you. Now just... breathe and... let go!

And by the way, I am assuming that you meant 'distance makes you grow fonder' when you wrote 'distance makes you grow fodder.' Because that is something that I have never heard before.

Take care.

Superna.

What the hell! Ok, she has no right to talk to me like that. I am gonna send her a rude mail back right now. No, wait. I should not do that. That would make her think that I am a total... lunatic. So I am just gonna do what she always does – not reply to her mail. Yes, I should completely do that. And in order to... distract myself, I should call up my friends and fix up a meeting with them. Yes, this makes complete sense – I think about Superna all the time because I don't have anything else to do these days. So all I need to do is... meet people, develop a social circle... and that's it! Life would be all happy again.

The way old friends do

I called all six of the numbers I found, and four times, I got the message 'does not exist'. I was only able to get in touch with Akshay and Shubham. Akshay said he was really happy to hear from me and everything, but was busy, so could not meet. Shubham on the other hand, said that it would be great to meet up. So we fixed a meeting. In fact I am on my way to meet him right now – at this coffee shop. I reach the venue and standing in front of the glass door, I feel a rush – I can feel my life going back to what it used to be. The coffee shop meetings with friends are back – soon the rest is gonna follow. This is so much fun!

I push open the door and freeze there for a second. A feeling of shock hits me. This coffee shop is unlike any I have been to. It's crowded like crazy and is beyond noisy – it's deafening in here. I am just in time to spot a vacant table with some used dishes lying on it. Before anyone else could occupy it, I dash to the table, sit down, wave for a waiter and gesture for him to clean the table.

Ok, so I am five minutes early and very uncomfortable. I pick up the menu card just to pretend that I am busy reading it.

People here talk a lot. And God! Are these people loud or what? They are supposed to be talking but it seems more like they are screaming. The place is thundering with sounds. Seriously, it's not even funny. It's so noisy and disturbing, and I feel so… nervous and out of place that I could actually cry! Just look at those guys at that table. They look like some college kids with spiked hair and bright T-shirts. They are throwing balls of crushed paper at each other and are about ready to wrestle. Could things be more inappropriate? This is no nice, relaxing coffee shop. I think I should wait for Shubham and when he comes, we should just shift to a different venue.

Oh! There he is. Great! He stands at the door, looks around, spots me, waves and walks over.

"Hi" he says as we shake hands and get seated.

"How are you? Long time!" he says.

"Yeah, long time indeed. 10 years I think, right?" I smile.

"Ya, it must be close to 10 years."

A moment of awkwardness follows. We both look at each other and observe. I don't know why the expression on his face changes, but it's really awkward looking at him. First of all he doesn't look like anything I remember from school. He has grown quite... fat and has developed a very distinct and identifiable paunch. Half of his head has gone hairless. The skin on his face has grown loose and he definitely does not look like he is in his 20s.

"This place does not serve the best coffee. Do you mind if we go somewhere else?" he asks me.

"Oh no, no. Not at all!" I blurt out instantly. Thank God!

We move out of the coffee shop and I follow him to the parking lot where he had parked his *WagonR.*

"I know of a great vendor who serves the best coffee," he says as he drives.

"Great!" I say.

"So tell me, what are you doing these days?" he asks.

"Well... these days, I am... trying to figure out what I should do..." I trail into silence.

He shoots me a look of extreme shock as if I had just confessed a murder.

"You mean you are not doing anything?"

"That's... another way of putting it..." I stammer.

"But *why*?" he looks at me again.

"Well... I have just spent some time pursuing the career that I chose when I was in *school*, and it turns out that I don't find it particularly exciting. So... I am thinking of... shifting. Yes."

"But how can you just... waste all the time you have spent in college studying? I am sorry but that does not sound like the best thing to do." He shoots me a look again, only that the look is accompanied by a frown this time.

"I don't know... it's just that a career is what keeps a person busy for most of his life.And how can one spend his life doing something that he doesn't enjoy? Something that... does not... satisfy? And moreover, I don't think that I am wasting my education. When I was in college, they taught me not only the principles of architecture, but also the principles of... life, and design. They taught me how to understand things – how to understand myself. More than anything else, it was a training period to develop a thought process. I don't think I am wasting any of that," I say.

He looks at me again with a bad frown. Ok, now it's getting irritating – he should focus on driving and quit turning his head like that.

"You have been watching a lot of movies haven't you? Those three idiots have spoiled it for everyone, haven't they?"

I look at him perplexed.

"No, that is not true. That idiot, I mean... that movie has got nothing to do with my decision whatsoever. It's just how things... turned out," I say.

"But why did you decide to come back?" he asks.

"I just fell very sick. And everyone at home said that I was not able to handle things on my own. So I was... brought back."

"Hmm, and with the recession on, it must have been difficult to hold on to the job as well, no?"

I WAS NOT FIRED!!! IWASNOTFIRED IWASNOTFIRED IWASNOTFIRED! God! This is so bugging! I should have videotaped the whole thing at the office and shown it to everyone.

But I don't have that. And I must say something. Because if I remain silent, he is gonna take it as the truth.

"No actually. They wanted me to stay. But I just felt that I needed time to gain my... good health back."

"Hmm" he utters as he brings the vehicle to a halt.

I look around and the place looks really deserted. There is one little *dhaba* kind of a place at the edge of the road and not a single soul in sight. This does not look like a happening place at all. Oh my God! Am I in trouble? Has this *'friend'* of mine turned into a... *psychopathic serial killer* over the years that we were not in touch? Is he gonna draw out a knife now and stab me, damaging my liver, or my heart or my lungs and push me out of the car and leave me here to bleed to death? I am sure no other car is gonna pass by on this road for another 15 minutes at least. By that time I would have passed out due to the pain and then would die and... never wake up! Oh no!

"Rishabh?"

"YA!" I almost leap in my seat.

"We are there," he says as he opens the car window.

"Yes, of course, we are there!" I say as I unbuckle the seat belt and get out of the car.

It's a very dark night and the breeze is cool – I can feel it rustling my hair lightly.

Beyond the *dhaba,* it seems like there is a piece of farmland along the edge of the road.

I turn around to locate Shubham and follow him as we both go and sit on a *charpoy.* (Yes, that is the furniture they have there.)

"So?" he looks at me and says.

"So," I reply as if in self defense. I sense another awkward question forming in his mind! I must say something before it rolls out of his mouth!!

"You tell me – what have you been upto?" I smile.

"Well, as you know, I got married, a year and a half back."

"I know. Congratulations once again." (As I say that, I have serious doubts as to whether or not it is an appropriate time to congratulate him – it's so late.)

"Thank you," he replies anyway. But I can sense that he is still cross with me for not attending his wedding. Yes, he did send me an invitation and I have been the (snobbish) one who has not made any effort to stay in touch. *But I don't like attending weddings!* They are such awkward affairs! But it would be of no use to explain that to him. And I don't think he'll be very amused if I tell him that I would have found *his* wedding awkward. If fact, I don't think anyone would like to hear that.

"And three months back, we had a baby girl," he continues.

"Oh wow! That is great. Congratulations... again."

Oh my God! His life is so over. I really feel sorry for him.

"Yes. Thanks. Life has changed in the past few years," he says. And as he says that, I can't help noticing the change in his appearance again. He looks like an uncle now, and there is no doubt about it.

"I used to wonder how life would be after marriage. And how it would... not be the best thing to have someone who clings to you in everything you do. You can't take decisions as freely as you could before. But frankly, I feel that things became a lot more beautiful after I got married. There is no other feeling like coming home to your wife at home after a long day at work. It just refreshes you, and completely... renews you." He says this with a bright smile.

"Hmm," I say as I stare at him, listening.

"And your whole... system changes." He continues, "I mean, if your wife wants a... diamond ring, you just... forget everything else – the things that you need, the things that you were planning to buy for yourself, and you just get down to it and start saving for her ring," he says smiling, looking at the ground.

Ok, this statement of his has complete potential to freak me out of my wits. But I must not let any such feeling surface. For he is gonna think that I am even more weird than I am sure I already appear to him.

He shoots me a look and continues, "And you really don't have a choice. Coz if you don't get what she asks for, there would be fights... and quarrels."

"Hmm..." I can't think of anything more than to keep humming hmm. Just then a shabbily dressed young boy who must not be older than 12 appears by our side.

"Two coffees," Shubham orders.

I look at him as he walks away.

"That kid is too young to work," I say.

"Yes, there must be some unavoidable circumstances at his place."

Hmm, someday I would like to talk to one such kid and know what is it that forces them to work like this.

"So?" he says again.

"So, tell me. What are you doing these days?" I ask him before he can say anything else.

"I am handling my Dad's factory these days. You know we had a plastic manufacturing unit, right?"

"Oh yes. I know, I remember." I had no clue about it whatsoever.

"I am telling you dude, you too must get married."

"I don't know... how can I think of getting married when I am not even settled in life? Like... I don't even know what I want to do in my life. How can I take up the responsibility of marriage in such a state?" Yeah, I think to myself, I don't have my Dad's *factory* to take care of that would bring in all the finance I need to run a house. But how would he understand that?

"All that takes care of itself. But seriously man, you should get married soon. And whether you accept it or not, the age factor is also there."

I stare back at him completely motionless and wide-eyed. What is wrong with him? Why is he making us sound like we are 40!

"No, seriously. All the young girls, let's say 21, 22 year olds, they are gonna find you too old for them."

That would seriously be very good. Because I, in any case, do not wish to marry a girl who is still in college.

"And dude, I must tell you, there is no greater joy than holding your own child in your arms. I feel we humans were put on this earth only to experience that."

Just then that 12 year old boy comes and places two hot, steaming cups of coffee in front of us.

The orange hangover

⌐← **Natasha is online.**

Rishabh – there is something seriously wrong with this town. everyone believes that as soon as you hit 25, you are just supposed to get married, grow fat, start balding and... make babies!

Natasha – O God! please! chill.

Rishabh – did you get my mail about the meeting with my friend?

Natasha – yes i did.

Rishabh – so?

Natasha – so?

Rishabh – so what do you have to say about it?

Natasha – you really want to listen?

Rishabh – yes i do.

Natasha – grow up.

Rishabh – sorry?

Natasha – you got it right.

Rishabh – :/

Natasha – when are you going to understand other people's perspectives?

Rishabh – ok, why don't you go all judgmental after you listen to how the meeting with my *second* friend went?

Natasha – go on.

Rishabh – so I went to meet akshay (he was finally able to take some time out from work btw).

Natasha – ok.

Rishabh – and he is not married yet, so i thought that he would not have the same old stories to tell about his wife and how she wants a diamond ring and how his life completely revolved around it now.

Natasha – hmm

Rishabh – we started talking general stuff, what he had been up to all these years, and what I had been up to and stuff.

Natasha – k

Rishabh – and then he asked me the most obvious question – do i have a girlfriend.

Natasha – hmm

Rishabh – i said no (as i didn't want to appear like a loser telling him about superna) and then i asked him the obvious question back.

Natasha – k

Rishabh – and he said no too.

Natasha – good.

Rishabh – and then he started telling me about his 'sex adventures'.

Natasha – God save me!

Rishabh – precisely. he started telling me that he had never had a girlfriend but had made out with girls quite a few times. he said it was easy to get one as all one had to do was pay a few bucks.

Natasha – that's nothing new.

Rishabh – ya, but what was new was how he explained the kind of things that those girls did, and how they did it and how dirty and unhygienic the whole thing felt and-

Natasha – rishabh, stop it! I don't want to listen to all the gory details.

Rishabh – ya, even i don't want to remember all that.

Natasha – cut cut cut, change topic.

Rishabh – my puppy ran away.

Natasha – LOL, you are never short of topics, are u? anyway, why did it run away? you refused to give it the diamond ring it asked for is it?

Rishabh – won't you ever stop making fun of me?

Natasha – i am not making fun of you. i was just joking, and you know that. now don't get all serious and touchy about it and tell me how you lost the puppy.

Rishabh – i did not feed him on time. i can't even take care of a puppy and make it stay with me! i am doomed for life! no girl is ever gonna settle with me and i am gonna be lonely for life.

Natasha – …yawn…

Rishabh – natasha, it's a major life crisis here! and this is how you respond?

Natasha – what should I do? I know you are not gonna follow what i am gonna say.

Rishabh – that is not true.

Natasha – that is so true.

Rishabh – no it's not.

Natasha – you have had enough rest and you need to take up a job now.

Natasha – what happened now? why have you fallen silent?

Rishabh – i have not fallen silent, i was just... thinking.

Natasha – thinking of what? an excuse?

Rishabh – nooooo! anyway, forget it, you would never understand.

Natasha – there is nothing to understand. you are just a lazy bum and you don't ever want to work.

Rishabh – you would not understand coz you are happy with your job and good with your career choice. you work for a cause... you are getting what you want out of life.

Natasha – hmm, ok, so you suffer from 'The Orange Hangover'.

Rishabh – ?

Natasha – obviously you don't know what 'The Orange Hangover' is, it's a term that i have coined and don't you ever try to claim that you came up with it coz I would sue you then.

Rishabh – yeah, yeah. will you just tell me what it means?

Natasha – orange, the colour, is a mix of red and yellow. so it represents the fusion of its parent colours that represent passion and happiness. the colour (orange) also represents creativity, celebration, fascination, warmth, enthusiasm, optimism, determination, courage, energy, power, intellect, harmony and endurance. in short, it represents all the qualities and ideas that we are taught to imbibe as part of 'good living' as children in school. but most of us, when we step into the 'real world' (as some people want to call it) are forced to wash it all off. some people do that – successfully forget all of it and live a life of 'different values' as I like to think of it. but some people are not able to wash it all off themselves. some of these ideas, these values still cling to them. and these are the people, who I say, suffer from 'the orange hangover'.

Rishabh – wow! quite a thought there!

Natasha – i know. but anyway, what I wanted to say was that things will start working out only if you take a step. nothing will happen if you keep sitting like that.

Rishabh – but i need to take the step in the right direction. anyway, i am sleepy. catch u later. GN.

Natasha – yes, that's typical rishabh – if someone says anything you don't agree with, you go sleepy and say good night.

Rishabh – ☺ talk to you later.

Natasha – good night rishabh.

Rishabh – good night natasha.

The bitter bite

When one does not have a job, one does not really have a reason to get out of bed. I mean, I have been up for like a good 40 minutes or so now, but I'm feeling too lazy to get out of my bed. It's so nice to just lie in bed; why would anybody ever want to get out of it?

"Rishabh, are you gonna sleep the whole day?" My Mom is almost yelling outside the door of my room.

I stretch lazily and say, "I am not sleeping" as loudly as I can manage, being half asleep.

"Get up now!" she says as I hear her walk away.

Hmm, on second thoughts, maybe I should get out of bed. I am kind of hungry. And if I keep lying in bed and never get out, I will eventually starve and turn into a skeleton, meaning – I will die. And I don't want that to happen.

So I force myself to get out of the room and walk into the kitchen.

"What's for breakfast?" I ask Mom, rubbing my eyes.

"Leftovers from last night," she says flatly.

"What? I can't have that terrible *dal* and *bhindi ki sabzi* again!"

She turns around and says, "The kitchen is all yours."

"Fine" I say irritated, looking at her.

I think about it and decide to have eggs, I can make scrambled eggs, yes, those are easy. I can totally make scrambled eggs.

I pull open the fridge door and look around inside it. I don't see any eggs.

"Where do we keep eggs?" I ask Mom.

"We are out of eggs."

Isn't she bothered at all? Her son, her own *son*, is hungry. And all she has to say is 'we are out of eggs'? "Fine, I'll go get eggs," I say.

"Good," she says.

Doesn't she know? They don't distribute eggs for free in the market. They take money before they give you any. Why isn't she giving me money to get the eggs?

I look at her for a moment and she looks back at me blankly, so then I say, "Give me money." God, saying that takes me back to my teenage days, back to school days when I used to ask her for money whenever I had to go hang out with my friends or watch a movie.

She looks back at me and says; "You know your Dad was running his whole house when he was your age."

I really don't have anything to say but I still manage to say, very confidently, "Well, I am not my Dad." Completely aware that I look foolish saying that.

* * *

I feel curious walking on the street where, as a kid, I had celebrated numerous escapes in the afternoons when my mother used to threaten me in uncountable ways about what she would do to me if I went out in the afternoon to play. It's funny how certain memories refuse to fade irrespective of how old they are. Feeling completely nostalgic, as if right out of an old black and white movie (in which the hero comes back to his hometown after ages to see that everything is still the same) I enter the shop, buy the eggs and head back home. I simply can't help recalling the things I used to do as a kid. I remember the fruit vendor, whom I would go running to, asking for oranges. I must have been some... six or seven years old then. Such sweet oranges he would get, specially for me, with so much love. It would feel so nice. Everyone used to like me, *love* me; *everyone* – the neighbours, the shopkeepers... all of them. Why did I ever leave this place to earn money? Just then I see one of the neighbouring aunties coming out of her house with her son. God! How big he has grown! I remember him being a little kid when I went to college, leaving this town. I feel so wonderful seeing that aunty. I remember she would always bring me a Five Star bar of chocolate each time she came to our place when I was a kid. I simply can't stop myself from walking over to say 'hi' to her.

"Hello aunty," I say. She is startled, she did not see me coming.

Immediately she looks at her son and whispers in his ear, *"Go inside, he is a bad influence, the one who quit his job and is sitting at home idle."* Without a word, the son goes inside.

I don't even get a chance to say 'hi' to him or ask him what he is doing these days.

The aunty looks at me and smiles. She thinks she was not audible.

"Hello beta, how are you?" she says, all gleaming.

I feel a punch of disgust in my gut. Why the hell is everyone in this place so judgmental? I don't even want to speak to her.

"I am good Aunty, how are you?" I force myself to say.

"I am good. I got to know you came back a few days ago. How's everything going?"

"Good, Aunty, everything is good."

"I heard you don't want to practise architecture," she says, giving me a look.

I simply smile.

"So you are gonna waste five years of your studies," she continues.

"Not really Aunty, it was a very good course that taught me a lot of things. It –"

She cuts me off and says, "But they basically taught you to make buildings, didn't they?"

I realize there is no point explaining.

"Yes Aunty," I say.

There is an awkward silence and I finally manage to say,

"I got to go Aunty, this needs to reach the kitchen ASAP," and I show her the bag of eggs I am holding.

"Sure" she smiles, "do come over sometime." She smiles again.

Yeah, *sure*. I just nod and smile back. Huh! As if!

As I walk away I hear a very familiar sound.

"*Kinnu leoooooooo.*"

It's the fruit vendor, unmistakably, it's him. I can never, ever forget his calls. Suddenly images of him pushing his cart and entering the street flash in front of my eyes and I am overcome by nostalgia.

I look at him, smile and wave. He waves back at me, pushes his cart speedily in my direction. So maybe there are some people who still like me a lot.

He comes to a halt right next to me and has a slight look of distress on his face.

"Hey, Rishabh, how are you?" he asks.

"I am good," I smile, "how are you?"

"Very good," he says as he takes a pause and observes me.

Awkward silence.

"When are you getting married?" he asks.

Oh my God!

"No plans as yet," I force a smile.

"You should get married now, you are getting old," he says.

"Not that old," I say, "And what's the rush? We live in India, where one thing is completely certain – you will get married for sure."

"No, no, you must not delay," he insists.

Ok, this is getting weird – I see this fruit vendor after like a decade and he starts forcing me to get married, what's wrong with him?

I do not say a word and beam back at him. I am telling you, small towns are not the most exciting places to be in if you are in your mid 20s.

"Get married!" he repeats, almost as if it was an order.

"I will" I say, "But I have to go right now." He is still looking at me as I start to walk away. Then suddenly it strikes me and I turn around and ask, "Can you please get oranges for me tomorrow?"

"Yes, I will get them," he says, with the look of worry still alive on his face.

It's not my fault – I am not a bad person!

I enter the kitchen totally depressed, put the eggs on the kitchen counter and start walking to my room.

"You will need to make your breakfast yourself," Mom calls.

"Not really hungry, I'll have breakfast later," I reply and continue walking.

I can almost feel her turning her head and looking at me. After a few seconds I hear,

"Come here, I want to talk to you." And it's not her usual tone that sounds like an order. There is a strong note of concern that I can sense in her voice, she knows I am upset. And there is no denying that I do feel terrible right now. I could surely use a little pep talk. My shoulders slumped, I go and sit on the vacant chair next to her. It still is a beautiful morning and bright, warm, golden light is filling the room. I look outside the window and see the green grass glistening in the morning sun and then I look at my Mom.

"Someone said something?" she asks looking into my eyes.

"No" I shake my head.

"Good, because I would have beaten the life out of any person who did," she says in a strong voice. I never told you, but my Mom comes from a *royal bloodline*. We are descendants from the royal family of Chamba. My great-great-great-great Grandfather was the King of Chamba once upon a time. And I would have been the prince of Chamba today if the British had not come into the picture. I have fantasized about this ever since childhood; in fact, I still play act like the Prince of Chamba in front of the bathroom mirror at times. I have even made a few home videos in which I have dressed up like a prince and am conducting a court. But no one knows about the videos. And no one ever will – they are saved in my personal computer as 'hidden files' and I have a copy of them burned on a DVD but I have never told anyone where it's hidden.

After a few seconds of silence, she asks again, "Then what's the problem?"

"It's... the choices that we have to make... and it's not my fault..." I am so troubled that I can't even speak. I stammer and feel kind of scared that I am going to burst out crying any moment.

"Calm down, easy," she says, as she puts her hand on my knee and tries to comfort me.

"It's the choices that we have to make." I gather my courage and start again, "It's the fault of our education system. How can you expect a 12th standard kid to know what he wants to do for the rest of his life? When there is no exposure given to him, he has no idea about any profession, and he is asked to make a choice. I mean... just think about it, when in school, one is expected to just go to school, come back, study and get good marks. Yes one can get involved in sports to an extent but that's it. If he does anything else, he is a bad kid. This goes on till the 10th standard. And then he is asked to choose a stream of study - Medical, non-Medical, Commerce or Arts. If he has been a good kid, he should be able to take up Med or non-Med. If he has been average in his performance then Commerce, and if he was a total failure, then it's Arts for him. How can a... 16 year old kid make such a choice? He does not know anything... he does not even know himself well at that time. And then you are supposed to go to college and finish graduation. After that you are supposed to step into the real world and do what you have been trained for. And if you do not do so, you are a *bad person*!"

My Mom is looking at me intently as I am speaking and I can see warm sympathy in her eyes. I still have so much pent up inside me that I do not want to stop. "When you are a kid and you have all those dreams and you talk about them, people say 'this kid is gonna go places'. But when you grow up and talk like that, people say that you are mad and... hide their children behind themselves..." My eyes start to fill up as I say those last words. It was really humiliating how that aunty behaved with me. "It's not wrong to dream. It's not wrong to struggle to find what you really want to do for the *rest of your life*. How can I spend all my life doing something that I do not enjoy, that I do not *feel* passionately about? It's not a crime that I want to find the right thing for me. But why do people always keep judging?" My throat feels strained and I feel exhausted. I lean on the backrest of the chair and rub my head.

My Mom starts to say slowly, "Rishabh, you should not care about what people say. You should not get affected. It's *your* life, and *you* have the fullest right to take all the decisions. But yes, there are some responsibilities that come with life and one can't ignore them. I have said this so many times before, I'll say it again – maintain a balance. Do what you want to do but be a little practical too. I am not asking you to do something that does not thrill you, for the rest of your life. You must find your calling, you must chase what you are meant for. But till you find that, you can't keep sitting idle."

I look at her with an active whirlwind of thoughts inside my head.

"God, you are such a drama queen!" she says and lets out a sigh. Now she is back to her usual tone.

"Must have exhausted all your energy. Let me get some scrambled eggs for you," she says as she leaves for the kitchen.

Part II

A new day has come

There isn't any point in discussing it with anyone or asking for any more advice. I have created quite an issue of it already. So I am on my way for the interview. My Mom has been working on it for quite a while now it seems, highlighting all the *'Architect required'* ads in the newspapers with a bright green fluorescent marker. I hold the newspaper with the specially coloured ad beaming at me and look at the address mentioned in the ad. It doesn't look impressive. There is a row of shops that opens onto an arcade, which touches the footpath. I can see a *Bobby Hardware Store* and a *Lucky Photo Studio*. It's an old building that has not been painted in years. Next to a window on the first floor I see a board advertising the architect I am supposed to meet. The board is rusted and completely worn out – it can actually fall down any instant. But I am not going back without going through the interview. And that is not because I am desperate about the job, but because I love interviews. I believe that is the best part of a job – it's like the first date 'hello, how are you? Where are you from?' After that it's all work and responsibility and 'why did you do that?' and 'why didn't you do that' and all the other conflicts on earth.

I take a deep breath and head for the stairs.

* * *

I push open the heavy wooden door that reveals an office that looks like something that has been frozen in time. But it's not a bad feeling I get. It looks like something right out of the 70s and I have always had a major fascination for the decade. Though I was born a decade later, I still feel an uncanny connection with the time. I really don't know if it was the hippie-follow-your-will thing of that age or simply the fact that my parents got married in that decade, that binds me to it.

There is a row of chairs lined along the wall and a person who looks like a peon is sitting on one of them.

"I had an appointment for an interview," I say to him.

He nods and goes into another room.

I look around and observe the room keenly. There are heavy squarish wooden chairs with leather seats, a model of a house in one corner, placed on a pedestal inside a glass casing that does not look impressive and there are rows of pictures of houses pinned neatly on a soft board hung on the wall. I step closer to the board to study the style of the houses in the pictures. All of them look old, as if they are from the mid 70s or 80s with some artistic features (murals or motifs etc.) – the kind of houses we see in Hrishikesh Mukherjee's movies.*

It's a quaint feeling, looking at those pictures, almost like traveling back in time. I am so lost in thought that I am startled

---

* In his more stylish movies like *Gol Maal, Chupke Chupke* and the like.

by the squeaking of the door as the peon guy steps out.

"Sir has asked you to wait," he says.

Oh, ok. I thought I was on time.

And that is how it all went

Natasha: so finally! some sanity is creeping into someone's head.

Rishabh: ?

Natasha: as if you don't know what i am talking about. anyway, tell me, how did it go?

Rishabh: 15 minutes. *15* minutes! he made me wait for *15 minutes*!!!

Natasha: ok, then?

Rishabh: and i really got the feeling that during all that time he wasn't even busy.

Natasha: ok, then what happened?

Rishabh: i mean like... why would someone do that? why would he make me wait when he is not even busy?

Natasha: grrrrrr! ok, cut to – you open the door and enter the room. then what happened?

Rishabh: uh! you never listen to what i have to say.

Natasha: will you just get on with it?

Rishabh: huh! anyway. so i opened the door and went inside.

Natasha: thank god!

Rishabh: there was this one oldish guy. no, wait, he was not oldish, he was very *old*, he had totally gray hair and wrinkled skin. god! I don't even want to imagine how old he must be!!! he was like ancient! the ancient dude.

Natasha: ok, then what happened?

Rishabh: he must have been 65, or 70.

Natasha: ok, he was an old man with gray hair, what did he do?

Rishabh: he looked at me as he raised his right eyebrow and asked me to sit.

Natasha: v. good. then?

Rishabh: there was an awkward silence for a while and then he asked for my resume.

Natasha: k

Rishabh: so i handed it over and he stared at me. gosh! he read it as slowly as he was old. he took such a long time to read that i started to wonder that what the hell i had written in there! i mean there is hardly anything on my CV!

Natasha: hmm

Rishabh: and then after like a 1000 hours he looked up and asked – 'so you were working in gurgaon.'

'yes sir' i said. then he asked, 'why did you leave?' and i said 'i fell sick, sir.' then he fell silent and after a few seconds, he said, 'yes, with the recession, it must have been difficult for them to hold the job for you too.' and then i said —

Natasha: rishabh i don't want you to start ranting about the 'i was not laid off' thing again. PLEASE!

Rishabh: ok ☺

Natasha: yes, now go on.

Rishabh: and then there was this general talk about what projects i have worked on, what are my 'other interests' and stuff, and then he started talking.

Natasha: k

Rishabh: he said that he wasn't looking for just an employee, but he was looking for a partner who could handle his office as he kind of wanted to retire. he wanted someone to take care of his office completely.

Natasha: hmm.

Rishabh: and he said that i looked just like his son.

Natasha: oh god!

Rishabh: i know!! it's like a freaking coincidence!!!

Natasha: and where is his son by the way?

Rishabh: he is in the US somewhere, he is settled there.

Natasha: are you joining?

Rishabh: after one week.

Natasha: and what do you need that week for?

Rishabh: ? I'm going to soon be stuck in that working routine. i want to relax for at least a week before i give it all up!

Natasha: lazy bum!

Rishabh: you would never understand, natasha.

Natasha: anyway.

Rishabh: whatever. : x

Natasha: and are you over that orange man incident?

Rishabh: i guess, i am quite over the trauma.

Natasha: but you know something, you should be open to the idea of meeting people.

Rishabh: …what do you mean?

Natasha: arranged marriage ain't the best way these days you know.

Rishabh: marriage is not on the cards right now.

Natasha: anyway, forget it did you settle your salary package with you new 'old' boss?

Rishabh: …not technically, but he said that he would give me the best in the market.

Natasha: god! no wonder he said you look like his son.

Rishabh: what do u mean?

Natasha: oh god rishabh, would you ever learn?

* * *

I wake up in the morning completely tired. I have not been able to sleep even for a minute. I just could not get Superna out of my head. Why does everyone keep asking me to be 'open' and 'receptive'? I am gonna end up with her; it's just a matter of time before things settle. No, that is not true; actually... deep down I know that things are over. God! And as this thought surfaces in my mind, I suddenly feel dizzy. There is no way I can even imagine my life alone – how would I ever live without her! But anyway I pull myself out of the bed and walk out of my room. Mom is already sitting at the breakfast table, having an apple.

"What's for breakfast?" I ask rubbing my eyes.

"Scrambled eggs. What else do you expect, *shahi paneer*?" she says as she gets up to fix me breakfast.

I slump down on a chair and stare at the fruit bowl with unseeing eyes. After a few minutes, the fruits in the bowl actually catch my eye. Along with *cheekoos* and apples, there are oranges, nice, big, bright and tempting oranges. I pick one up, peel it and start eating it. God! The taste of a ripe, juicy, sweet orange!!! It's divine! You know something? I guess the Orange Man and Natasha were right, maybe I should be open to the idea. Maybe I should be more receptive.

Meeting a new girl

It's a weird town I tell you, you call your friends and suggest meeting up and they respond in the weirdest of ways. There's this girl I made friends with on Facebook a long time ago when I was in college. Her name is Janvi. She was studying architecture back then (at C.C.A.*) and needed some information on green buildings and sustainable architecture. I helped her with that, and ever since then, we have been in touch (via Facebook). I have never seen her – she never puts her own picture on FB. She always has pictures of various kinds of landscapes and stuff as her profile picture and she has zero albums. Anyway, I called her up and fixed a meeting. There was some problem with the phone connection and the signal kept breaking off, but I clearly heard her saying that it would be great to meet up as we both were finally in the same city and that her *Masi* would come along. Now I really don't get why she wants to bring along her *Masi*. Anyway, let's see how it goes.

* * *

For 15 minutes now I have been sitting here waiting – alone. She has called 3 times since I have reached and apologized like some 20 times already. There is hardly any activity around. I had deliberately chosen this time – 3:3o p.m. – total off time, no one thinks of going out for a coffee around this time. I force my eyes back to the pages of the book that I'm pretending to read to look busy and occupied. I try reading the book – *The Palace of Illusions*. It's an adaptation of the greatest epic ever written – the *Mahabharata*. (Actually it's not the book I am reading these days. The book that I am *actually* reading is *Diary of a Wimpy Kid*. It's the funniest book I have read in years. Why I am sitting here holding another book, *pretending* to read it is because I know for a fact that girls love it when guys read *serious* and *cultural* stuff. No grown up guy can ever impress a girl by telling her that he reads *The Wimpy Kid*.) Looking at the pages of the book in my hand, I continue wondering why her aunt is coming along with her! She said that she has seen my picture on FB and can recognize me,

---

* C.C.A. = Chandigarh College of Architecture

but can she really? I mean, I look fatter in my pictures – the camera adds 10 pounds (we all know that). What if she comes, looks at me, does not like me and leaves. I wouldn't even know that she ever came – *I have no idea what she looks like!* It's almost like a blind date and something inside me starts to jump with anxiety. Not only because I feel insecure about the way I look, but also because somewhere deep down, I feel that I am cheating on Superna. I should not go around meeting other girls. That would be no good for our relationship. I know Natasha keeps telling me that there isn't any relationship left anymore, but I know that it's only a little confusion which I am soon gonna clear and then everything will be fine. Hmm, but if that is the case, then what the hell am I doing sitting here, waiting to meet someone I have never, ever seen before? I should just get up and leave. Yes, I should do that. I put the book back in my bag and take out my phone and am about to dial Janvi's number to inform her that we won't be able to meet, when suddenly I hear a voice above my head.

"Excuse me."

I look up to see who it is.

"Rishabh, right?" a girl asks. With her is another girl. Both of them look about the same age. I immediately figure out that it's Janvi. But who is the girl with her? It cannot be her aunt. And if she *is* her aunt, she is *very* young. I look at her for a moment. She is not only young but very beautiful too. She is tall and has a very nice and slender figure, and straight, shoulder length hair. Her eyes are big and round.

"I am *so* sorry for being *so* late; I see you were going to call me again," Janvi says and now I can also recognize her voice.

"Yes," I say as I force an awkward smile. I must not let her know that I was about to leave.

"I am so sorry," she repeats and sits down on a chair in front of me.

"It's ok," I say, maintaining my smile.

She smiles back as she takes her bag off her shoulder and puts it on the chair next to her. She looks at the girl who is with her and says, "Sit Mansi, why are you still standing?" and Mansi gives her an awkward smile. Suddenly the expression on Janvi's face changes and she looks as if she has committed a terrible blunder. She suddenly jumps up from the chair and says, "I am really sorry. I have such bad manners to impose myself like this. I mean... I sat down just like that even before you asked me to." And she picks up her bag from the chair in one quick motion. I cannot make full sense of what is happening but I stand up and say, "Come on, you don't need to be so formal. Please sit."

"Thank you," Janvi says as she throws the bag onto the chair again and sits down. Trying to contain her laughter, Mansi sits down next to her.

There is a moment of awkward silence, as no one knows what to say. I look at Mansi then look at Janvi and then look at Mansi again and ask, "Your *Masi*?"

"Yes, she is Mansi, but not *my* Mansi. Why would she be my Mansi?"

"I thought you said that *Masi* was coming with you... like... your aunt – *Masi*."

She breaks into a snort, "Why on earth would I want to bring my *Masi* along when I come to meet you? What's wrong with you?"

She suddenly stops laughing and looks horrified. "Oh my God!" she says, "I haven't even introduced you both." She looks at Mansi and says, "Mansi, this is Rishabh. We met on Facebook a couple of years back and since then we have been *terrific* friends." Then she looks at me and says, "Rishabh, this is Mansi, my cousin."

Oh, so it was *Mansi*! Stupid phone signals.

"Hi," I look at her and smile.

"Hi," she smiles back in a stunningly elegant way. There is a moment of connection as my eyes meet hers when we are interrupted.

"So, what's up? Who has coffee at this hour of the day?" Janvi asks.

"It's not that I like having coffee at this hour, it's just that... things are a little more peaceful around this hour at... such places."

"Oh my God you sound just like Mansi!" she bursts out saying.

Huh? What does she mean?

"Sorry?" I ask.

"What I mean is you are just like Mansi. She also does not like places that are too crowded. She also mentioned that she was relieved that we were meeting post lunch."

If she feels like that, then why won't Janvi let her say that herself. Can she not stay mum for like even a single minute?

"So we have something in common." I smile at Mansi again, "What do you do?" I try to strike up a conversation with her.

"She teaches in a school, primary section," Janvi butts in again.

Ok, it's getting irritating now. She is a teacher so she's definitely not dumb. She can speak. Why must Janvi keep interrupting us like this?

"That is nice to know. It's really a very noble profession." I look at Mansi and smile again, "What school?" I ask.

Her lips finally part and I hear her voice, "Apeejay."

"That is really nice to know," I say enthusiastically.

"What are you doing these days?" Janvi asks me.

"I just joined an office – "

"Really? Which one?" Janvi cuts me off.

"I will be working with Ar. Amandeep Randhawa."

"Oh my God! Really? It's not a nice office."

"Why do you say that?" I ask with a forced, worried laugh.

"No one lasts long there. They say there is something about that place. Anyway, how does that matter. Shouldn't we order some coffee now?"

Another suitcase in another hall

I push open the door and enter the office only to find it empty – there isn't a single soul around. Completely clueless as to what I should do, I walk in with timid, unsure steps. Standing in the middle of the room, I wonder if I am supposed to sit down, or just stand there, or go back or... do something that I can't think of. Have I reached too early? I look at my watch and it's 11:00 a.m. No, it's definitely not 'too early'. Just then I am startled by another voice in the room,

"Sir has left a sketch for you. He has asked you to start drawing it."

I turn around to see a guy standing at the door – darkish complexion and six to seven inches shorter than me*. From his looks, I can tell that he is the caretaker of the place.

"Great, so I have been hired." I smile.

"Ji?"

"Nothing," I say instantly, forcing an awkwardly serious expression on my face.

"Where is the workstation?" I ask.

"Ji?"

"I mean the computer."

---

* I am six feet tall by the way.

"Ji?" What's wrong with this guy? Is he programmed to answer only limited questions and if anyone asks anything else, he only says 'ji?'

I clear my throat and ask again, "I mean, where is the computer on which I will be working?"

"There are no computers here. All drawings are made on tables."

What?!

Ok, I am sure that I heard something wrong. It's the 21st century we live in. No one does manual drafting anymore. Maybe he has given me only partial information. Maybe he meant that there is another table *on* which there is a computer that I am supposed to work on. He starts walking out of the room and I follow him through an open corridor into another room. And what I see there is surely the one of the most horrific sights my eyes have ever beheld. The room is actually a studio unlike any I have seen before. It has seven or eight drafting tables most oddly set with no one working at them!

No, no, no! This is not real! I have not drafted a single line by hand for over six years! We stopped hand-drafting while we were in college itself – from the third year onwards! God! I am going into flashback mode... I remember how we had to bend down and draft on those tables for hours and hours and our backs would ache like crazy and we would get nightmares that we were gonna develop hideous hunches on our backs and look like the *Hunchback of Notre Dame*! No, no, no!!!

Ok, wait. I must not freak out. This must be part of a 'ragging' ritual they have here for newcomers. Like in my previous office they asked me to make coffee on my first day there and said that it tasted worse than dish water, and then when they saw how upsetting I found the comment, they all started laughing and got a nice big cake for me to cut and welcomed me to their office wholeheartedly. Yes, that is what it is – a 'ragging' ritual. And this must be the museum room in the office, used to show people or... students of architecture how it used to be in the olden times. I am sure all the other employees are giggling away to glory even as they are looking at my terrified expression from their hiding places. Any instant they are all gonna jump out and scream 'FOOLED YOU!' or something similar and then take me to where the nice new computers with up-to-date LED screens are all set neatly – where I am supposed to *work*.

Just then the caretaker taps my shoulder, hands me the hand-drawn sketch the boss has left, and leaves me staring at him as he walks out.

Damn it!

The new ancient office

I am stuck! I am stuck in an out-of-date office that smells terrible because of the ammonia fumes that are hanging in the air because of the fresh ammonia prints the caretaker just took. And there is no one else in the studio – *no one*, apart from the lizard that lives behind the blueprint machine that looks like a dried up twig (out of ammonia poisoning maybe) and comes out occasionally to peep at me and then goes back into hiding. Oh no! These fumes are gonna turn me into a twig-like figure too! Soon I am gonna start looking like the lizard!!! I am doomed! Why did I ever come here?

The caretaker comes and places a glass of water on the side table next to me. This is my chance! I must get some information from him before he disappears again.

"What's your name?" I turn to him and smile pleasantly.

After spending around 15 seconds in apprehensive confusion, he says, "Ram", and after another 5 seconds or so, he says, "Ram Savaray."

"Who else works here?" I ask.

"Sir comes in the afternoon at 2 o' clock. He goes back at 5 o' clock."

"Really? He doesn't come in the morning?"

"No."

"Why?" The question flew out of my mouth totally involuntarily.

"He sleeps very late in the night. He sleeps at 5 o' clock."

"You mean 5 o' clock in the morning?"

"Ji."

"Where are you from?"

"U.P."

"Where in U.P.?"

"Behraij Zila."

"I haven't heard of it. Where is it?"

"Zila Behraij, Thana Ram Gaon, Post Methaka, Mauja Jabdi, Gaon Jasmelpur."

"Wow! Must be some place. Are you married?"

"Ji."

"You have any children?"

"One son."

Suddenly I feel awkward for interrogating him like that (and also I have run out of questions).

"Do you want anything else?" he asks.

I shake my head and say, "No, thank you so much."

He walks out of the studio and I get back to my drafting table and start drafting again when my phone starts ringing.

'Natasha calling...' the screen flashes.

"Hi." I take the call.

"How's it going?"

"Hmm, it isn't like anything I had imagined."

"Why?"

"Shocker number one, there are no computers here – I have to draft everything manually."

"Ok."

"Shocker number two – I am the only employee."

"Hmm."

"Shocker number three – my boss is a creature of the night. He does not sleep in the night and comes to office only for two hours in the afternoon. He is a vampire of sorts – just like they show in the movies."

"Wow! That's really an interesting office."

"*Please*! Working here... feels like *time travel*! Sitting in this age old studio that is straight out of the 70s and making these drawings actually using ink and... locally made, cheap Isomars for good quality, nice, proper Rotring Isographs. It's totally like I have travelled back in time. God! Einstein would be so proud of me."

"Hmm, I have a feeling that Leonardo would be more proud of you," she says.

"Huh? Why would Leonardo Di Caprio be proud of me? It's not like I have gone back in time and am travelling on the *Titanic* and drafting drawings there."

I hear her letting out a sigh before she says, "I mean Leonardo Da Vinci would be proud of you as you are using such old instruments. But... anyway, on a serious note, I think you need to find your purpose there – there has to be a reason why you have ended up in this office."

I can hear Natasha saying something but I have drifted off elsewhere with my thoughts.

"Hmm, travel, I really wish I could travel to some place far away."

"Where? To a galaxy far, far away?"

"Hmm, and you know who else has travelled so far away? Superna."

"Oh my God! Please don't go there."

"You never listen to anything I have to say."

"That is not true, but I am not gonna argue with you on that. Tell me how the meeting with your Facebook friend went?"

She does not say it, but I know that she is asking this because she really wants me to forget Superna.

"The meeting went well. Although things didn't really click that well with Janvi. But I got along real well with Mansi, who, by the way, was her cousin and not her *Masi*."

"Ok, that's good. So what all did you guys talk about?"

"We didn't really get to talk much actually. Janvi kept interrupting all the time."

"So you guys didn't get to talk."

"Yeah, not really."

"And you are still saying that you guys got along well."

At times I really feel dumb when I talk to Natasha. I try to find an explanation and say, "What I meant was…" and I trail off into silence.

She starts laughing and says, "I was just pulling your leg. I understand you both felt a connection."

"Yes, thank you!" I say.

"And about your thing with Superna and the whole angle, the only thing I have to say about it is – you *can't make* someone fall in love with you. You can't force someone to stay with you. And even if you succeeded, it would never last. Now please mind it; this is the last time I am ever commenting on it. And you can note it down somewhere if you want and paste it on a wall somewhere, where you can look at it all the time and let it seep into your bony head."

"Hmm" is all I say, sitting motionless and thinking about what she just said.

Where do I belong?

God! Do I feel tired! I reached home at around 7:30 p.m. and saw today's episode of *The Vampire Diaries*, (yes, that's *the* thing to watch on TV these days – vampires rock!) had dinner, and now am lying on my bed. My back is aching like crazy and I want to do nothing but go to sleep. Manual drafting is so tiring, it's not even funny. Anyway, I need to stop thinking about the terrible shocks I received today and instead, relax. And so I decide to listen to the radio. I love the idea of music lulling me to sleep. I surf the channels and a somewhat pleasant tune catches my attention. It's a Punjabi song and it sounds nice. I decide to let the song play and crash on my bed. It's a rather nice song, I try to catch the refrain – *Paani Punjan dariyavan wala nehri ho gaya...* the song is really melodious. I close my eyes and lose myself to the song as I try to understand and feel the meaning of the words. It talks about how the water of the five rivers of Punjab had lost itself to tiny streams and hence lost its path. It talks of a boy who came to a big city from a village and lost all his values. The song is sung so powerfully that it hits me really hard and I feel beyond overwhelmed. I get flashbacks of everything that has happened to me in the past few weeks – meeting my friends, not being able to relate or to understand their values, the encounter with the aunty on the street who frantically wanted to hide her son from me, the strong reactions of the orange man... everything. I too have crossed cultures. I went from a small town to a big city. My whole value system and beliefs were altered. I am no longer who I used to be. *I* am the water of the five rivers that has lost its path. I have lost it all, I have changed. And I no longer fit here – I don't like anything here. I don't like anything about the very place that I was so fond of when I was younger – the place where I grew up, where I learned to stand up and walk. I feel terrible. I am a really terrible person – for I don't like the place that is the reason for my existence. My eyes start to well up as all these thoughts whirl around inside my mind with the song still playing on the radio pushing me further. Tears start to stream down my face and touch my ears and I don't know when I fall asleep.

What was I supposed to do?

It's not all that bad – to have a regular job and go to office every day. It fixes a routine for you, keeps you occupied during the day and does not let your mind wander off to places where it shouldn't go. I am thinking about this as I park my bike in front of the office building and stand and stretch for a moment, taking in a deep breath of the fresh, morning air. There is something in the air – I feel very... light today. I look all around and the hardware shop right below my new office catches my eye. There is a small kid sweeping the floor with a broom. It's shocking to see how child labour is so common in spite of all the laws. Terrible, *terrible!*

I pull out the keys from my bike and walk into my office.

Sitting on the bar stool, I try drafting but the cheap ink pen just won't work. I shake it, dab it – try everything but these cheap pens, they are good for nothing. It only loses its stubborn attitude after I completely dismantle the instrument, spill a few drops of ink on my jeans (accidentally), wash each and every part of it thoroughly and re-fill it with ink.

I have been working for over an hour now and I feel it's not all that tough – hand-drafting. It's more of a physical task and reduces one's chances of developing a paunch. Whereby, in turn, I can eat more of all the stuff that I like, that some people call 'junk food'.

I am quite engrossed in my work when I hear a sharp, long cry.

Is it Gabru Chotta Kutta Young??!! Did he actually find me and follow me all the way here and is now calling me because he wants me to take him back home? I feel a sudden strong urge to rush outside and see the dog. But wait a minute, I can't do that. I am the only employee in this office and need to... *man the office.* I immediately dash out of the studio and look for Savaray. He is sweeping the floor in the boss' room and has kept the dustbin on the boss' chair. It's a terrible thing to do but frankly, right now I really don't care.

"Savaray, there is a dog downstairs who is crying. It's my dog!" I say, sensing a deep and most awkward emotional tone in my voice. "I want you to go and bring that dog here."

I really don't know what I am thinking, I have no idea where I'll hide the dog. But I just can't leave the poor thing out on the road like that, again.

He nods and walks out. I go back to the studio and start pacing up and down impatiently.

After a minute or so, Savaray comes and stands in front of me. But there is no dog with him.

"Sir, it was not a crying dog. It was a crying boy."

I try to gain my senses and struggle to understand the situation. Ok, so there is no dog Savaray has with him. It was not Gabru Chotta Kutta Young, it was a boy. This boy must be around eight or nine years old. I look at him closely and his face looks kind of familiar.

"He works at the shop downstairs," Savaray says and I quit fumbling in my mind to find the answer.

"His master was beating him. He spilled paint on the floor," he adds.

Both of them stand motionless and I don't know what to do.

* * *

Natasha: YOU DID NOTHING?

Rishabh: what did u expect? call the police and get him arrested?

Natasha: i would have done that but that is not what i expected *you* to do.

Rishabh: then?

Natasha: what do u mean, then? you should have talked to the shop owner, threatened him that if he did not let the kid go, you would report it to the police as child labour is very much illegal and then questioned him about why he beat up the kid.

Rishabh: k k

Natasha: God! you are such a hypocrite!

Rishabh: please! i am *not* a hypocrite. i am one of the very few genuine people around. why would you even say that?

Natasha: please rishabh, day and night you keep whining about how you want to work for a cause, that you want to work for the betterment of society, and when you actually come across a situation where you are supposed to stand up for a cause, you do NOTHING! you just walk out silently. God! This is really frustrating. do you know the kinds of things these kids are put through? they make them work like crazy, they beat them up, they make them steal stuff, and don't even get me started on child abuse. the kids are at such a tender age and these people who employ them just wreck their minds. God! i still can't believe you didn't do anything.

Rishabh: hey, i was in any case gonna go and talk to that guy tomorrow. as it is i was feeling so bad about the whole thing. and you are just thrashing me left, right and centre.

Natasha: you better go and talk to him tomorrow. otherwise you don't know how bad i am gonna be with you.

Rishabh: vasay, i thought it was gabru chotta kutta young when I heard him cry.

Natasha: rishabh, don't irritate me more!

Rishabh: k k

Natasha: i am logging off now.

Rishabh: k

Natasha: and i want the complete report tomorrow – what you did, what he said – everything. he does not know what he is dealing with this time.

Rishabh: k k

Natasha: bye

Rishabh: bye

⤷ **Natasha has signed off.**

Phew *that* was something.

The kind of love that makes you follow someone home

I wake up wondering why I feel restless and head to the kitchen. Rubbing my eyes, I ask Mom, who is already working in the kitchen,

"What's for breakfast?"

"The usual. But we are out of eggs. Please get some, there is money on the fridge."

I don't have the energy to think about what she says. I simply walk to the fridge, take the money and walk out. It's a sunny day outside. And I see a few dogs sitting on the footpath. One of them is brown. Once upon a time, I too had a brown puppy. I had named him Gabru Chotta Kutta Young. But it's kind of weird – I didn't really spend many days with him. Why do I miss him so much? Why do I feel so attached to him? Maybe it's true what they said in the Meryl Streep/Clint Eastwood movie, the one in which he is a photographer and comes to shoot some bridges. What was it called? *Bridges of Madison Square Garden* or something, can't really recall the name. Anyway, in that movie they said that love can't be measured in terms of time and stuff. At times one single day spent with someone you really love can carry you through the rest of your life most happily. I am thinking about all this when suddenly something comes and hit my legs. It's something soft that is still moving.

Oh my God! It's Gabru Chotta Kutta Young!!! He is licking my shoes and jumping all around me. He puts his forelegs on my left leg and jumps, trying to reach for my hands.

I look at his face and I see pure excitement in his shining eyes. There is so much… love. I have never seen such unadulterated emotion ever on a human face. Gosh! Am I happy to see him?! I pick him up and realize that he has grown a lot heavier. And neither is he used to being picked up any more – he is wriggling to get away. He reaches for my hands nudging them a little with his tiny, soft, moist nose implying that I should let him go.

I cannot stop looking at him. I want to take him home. I put him back on the ground and and point in the direction of my house looking at him, gesturing him to come with me. He continues to jump around with his eyes twinkling and tongue lolling out from his wide open mouth. Then he looks at me and the other dogs that are around him in the street as if to tell me that he is not coming after me. I want him to come home again, with all my heart, but he doesn't move. I take a few seconds to understand what is happening – he has found his family – he is a part of this pack now – he is not gonna leave them. I stand there looking at him unable to understand how I feel. I go to him, kneel down, pat him, hug him one last time and leave. God! Now there is nothing left for me to do anymore. (Other than go and buy eggs, of course.)

* * *

I put the eggs on the kitchen counter and start walking to my room.

"I could use a helping hand in the kitchen you know," I hear my Mom say sternly.

"I don't feel so well today," I say, as I turn around.

"Hey, what happened? Did someone say something again? I am so gonna set all these aunties right."

At times it amazes me – how protective she is about me.

"No one said anything." I smile back.

"Then?"

"Just some things that I need to settle... inside my head," I say.

I go to my room and sit on the low seat next to the window. The glass shutter of the window is shut and I can see myself partially reflected against the garden outside that is in full bloom, lush with green grass. My mind is unsettled by all the thoughts that are running around inside. And of all things, it's my longing for Superna that surfaces most strongly. Just then Mom comes and gives me a cup of tea and goes out without saying anything. I take a sip as I stare at my reflection. It's strange how at times we see things that are not there; just like a reflection – just like Superna's love for me – it does not exist. And no matter how much I lie to myself and others, it's never gonna happen, never gonna come back. And it's time that I come to terms with this fact. I cannot force someone to be with me. And then the playful face of Gabru Chotta Kutta Young appears in front of my eyes again. And I remember how he looked at me. There was ecstasy in his eyes. Yes, there was love. *But not the kind of love that would make him follow me home.*

My gaze shifts from my reflection to the garden outside. It is a bright day – birds are chirping and butterflies are fluttering around beautiful, colourful flowers. My eyes follow a yellow-coloured butterfly as it flies from one big, bright, purple dahlia to another. The garden looks beautiful today. And it has been like this – the butterfly has always been there, and the birds and the flowers. It's just that I never had the eyes to see the beauty. But now I do – and I feel free.

Part III

The kid

I reach office and the first thing I do is call Savaray and ask him to get the kid from the shop below.

"He is not there anymore," he says plainly.

Oh my God!!! The guy has killed him! The kid is dead and it's all my fault! God! How am I ever gonna live with this! If only I had been a little stronger yesterday. If only I had done something!

"I took the boy home," Savaray says, breaking my train of thought.

I look at him shell-shocked. Ok, the kid is not dead. This is brilliant news.

"I took him home. He stayed the night with me. In the morning I called his parents in the village and sent him home. It was an 8 o'clock bus. He will reach home by six in the evening 6 p.m."

I feel ashamed as I listen to him. He did what I was not able to do – he helped the kid. And I am the educated one and supposedly the more sensible one here.

"You talked to his parents?" I ask.

"Yes."

I look at him and see humanity in his eyes. It's the lower section of society that we deal with most insensitively, so often. And we fail to see that they are such nice people. This guy has saved the boy from that evil... villain and doesn't even feel that he did anything great. He behaves as if it was his duty to do that. Whereas people like me would not stop beating their own drum even if they save an injured bird or insect.

"Where do you stay?" I ask him. Not that I am gonna arrange a better accommodation for him, but I just... ask him that anyway.

"I stay with boss," he says.

"You mean *the boss?* Like my boss who comes here every day?"

"Yes."

Oh my God! I must never bitch with him! Not about the office, not about the boss. Never, ever!!

"That is very nice to know," I say forcing a smile. "How long have you been staying there?"

"14 years," he replies simply.

"WOW! That is *some* time."

With a proud smile he says, "I was nine years old when I came here."

Oh my God! Another case of child labour! My boss should be put in jail!

We stand there in awkward silence, as I don't find anything else to ask him.

"I will get tea for you," he says hospitably and goes out of the studio.

Must (not) burn the table

I have been in office for A full two hours and haven't drawn a single thing. I have been crazily messaging Mansi about absolutely random stuff. Things like,

"ha ha ha my boss is not in office."

To which she replies,

"Mine won't stop hovering above my head."

To which I reply,

"Oh no! Then he must have read the message."

She replies,

"I am a dead duck!!!"

Then I type,

"Ha ha ha"

And press send and realize that I wanted to ask her something, so I instantly start typing again,

"Which is your favourite old hindi movie?"

She replies,

"You tell me first."

I am almost about to type 'Guide' with 100 percent dreamy eyes but something stops me from doing that and I type,

"I asked first, so you tell first."

"Guide"

"Hey!!! That's my fav too." I jump with joy. This is really cool. We have the same choices too – we enjoy the same stuff!

"☺"

The sight of the smiley makes me smile. I sense that she was smiling when she sent it to me and that image of her smile in my mind makes me smile.

Just then I get another message.

"Boss giving me dirty look and passing comments lyk 'very busy today Mansi' with sarcastic smiles. Must get back to work."

To which I reply,

"Yes, I should also get back to work. Tc. Cu."

I haven't worked a bit since morning. And I need to distract myself from Mansi. So I put on my headphones and tune in to the radio on my phone. I surf all the channels and immediately recognize a song *Aaj phir jeenay ki tamanna hai* and can't resist messaging Mansi,

"Turn on the radio, 34.5 FM"

"☺ Ok."

After spending a few seconds in total anticipation, I type,

"Like the song?"

"☺ yes, thank you."

"☺ You are welcome."

Ok, now really need to get back to work. It's almost 1 p.m. and Boss is gonna be here in an hour. I pick up the pen and start to draft. I have drawn nothing beyond the four walls of a room when Savaray comes and interrupts,

"Sir has come. He is calling you."

Oh no he has come early today! I am totally doomed! *I* am a dead duck now! Good lord! What am I gonna do? I have nothing to show my boss by way of work today. God! I get up and walk towards the boss's room as I frantically search my mind for an excuse. What should I say? Should I say that I spilled water on the sheet and it got completely ruined and I had to start all over again so I still need time to complete the drawing? No! This is no good, what if he says that he wants to see the ruined sheet? No, no, no, this won't work. It got burnt! Yes, the sheet got burnt because of a tiny fire because I was… playing with matchsticks!!! Yes! He *can't* ask me to fetch the ashes as proof. God! No! What am I thinking? How can I think that he won't be mad at me for playing with matches in his studio? *And*, if there was a fire, then why wasn't anything else burnt? How come the drafting table is completely un-burnt? Maybe I should burn the drafting table a little. But meantime I have already reached Sir's room and there is no time to burn the drafting table.

I go inside the room and stand in front of the boss, meek as a sheep.

He looks at me and then looks back at the drawings that are placed in front of him on his table.

"There is a new project that we need to start working on," he says, without looking up from the drawings.

"Ok," I utter, nodding with a confused frown.

"You need to go with the contractor to the site tomorrow to measure up the place."

"Yes sir."

"What time should I confirm with the contractor?" he asks as he lets out a little cough.

What should I say? What should I say? Is this a trick question? I should say that my reporting time for office is good. Yes! That is what he wants to hear. Or does he want me to go earlier? How can I find out? I am freaking out standing in front of him and I don't even know when I say,

"10.30 in the morning would be good, Sir."

Damn! I have stated my reporting time!

"Ok. I'll inform him," Boss says without looking up.

I stand there for like half a minute before I realize that that is all and I am supposed to leave.

I turn around and start walking out of the room. God exists! *God exists*!!! He didn't ask me about the drawing! I won't have to burn the office now!

Let's *not* talk about sex, baby

I have reached the office and I am bang on time. In fact, I am early, by a full two minutes. Who says I am a lazy bum? I am totally proactive. My life is so much in control it's not even funny. I have a regular job and will get a salary on a regular monthly basis. I can totally take care of all my expenses now. And if all goes well, soon I will start supporting my whole family and will be the *provider* of the house. The mere sound of it is so cool; I can't even imagine how cool it will be when it actually happens.

I put my bag next to the drafting table in my studio and sit down. But wait a minute, I don't need to work on the drawing today. I am going to the site. And that is the only thing I am supposed to do today. (Wow!)

Savaray comes and places a glass of water on the table next to my drafting table.

I am in a totally good mood and I want to strike up a conversation with him. And I also want him to open up a bit with me. It would be nice to know someone from a different culture. And he is a nice person too. I can't forget what he did for that kid.

"How are you Savaray?" I ask.

"I am good." He grins back.

"So, what's up these days? How's everything at home?"

"Everything is good."

"How's your son?"

"Good sir," he says as he sits down on a stool next to me.

"What's his name?" This is working. He is responding well.

"Krishna. But we are thinking of changing his name."

"Why? It is such a nice name!" I ask surprised. It *is* a nice name. Why would he want to change it?

"It does not sound good like other's children's names."

"I think it's a very nice name and you should not change it."

Most obediently he nods and says, "Ok."

Ok, now the moment of awkward silence has arrived and I struggle to find something to say.

"How's your wife doing? What's her name?"

"Manju," he replies, and then gives out a naughty little laugh. "You know, last night, we had a lot of *fun*."

…Ok, if I am sensing correctly, I don't want to go ahead with this.

"There is only one bed in our room. And I always sleep on the bed and she sleeps on the floor. Last night she said that her back was aching and she wanted to sleep on the bed. So I asked her to come and sleep on the bed with me. And then, she just touched me –"

"Ok, ok!" I cut him off. He is just gonna start with all the details and I don't want to get grossed out like that first thing in the morning. God! I did want him to open up to me, but not *so much*!

Then suddenly something strikes me.

"Where was Krishna at that time?"

He lets out a similar laugh again and says, "He was sleeping on the floor."

Good lord! Who knows if he was sleeping? He is about three years old (as per what Savaray says). What if he was not sleeping and was simply watching them both... do it. I mean look at how excited he is just telling me all this. Trying to imagine his excitement while... doing it, I can very well sense that he would never, ever notice it even if his son was watching them both. God! This is so irresponsible of them.

I just open my mouth still trying to figure out how should I explain it to him that he must take care not to... do all this in front of his kid, when I see a huge, fat man standing in the doorway. He has really big eyes and his skin is really dark. As if it's been burnt in the sun or something.

God! He is a robber! A Beagle Boy Robber! He has come in broad daylight to rob this office!!! Oh my God! He would have weapons – dangerous, deadly weapons!!! Where should I hide? Where should I run??

"Please come contractor *saab*," Savaray goes and greets him, "Should I get water?"

Phew!

The new people

The car that we are in comes to a halt (the one the client has sent for us) and does not even honk. A guard comes running and opens the gate and the car proceeds to the driveway and stops below a porch. The driver opens the door on his side, rushes out of the car and runs to the door by my side and opens it. In the most aristocratic manner I step out of the car followed by the contractor. That is when I see someone approaching us. He looks like a man in his 40s. He is tall and well-built – broad shoulders and no paunch whatsoever. He is wearing a white *kurta pajama*.

"Mr. Rishabh, welcome. Please come in," he says as he shakes hands with me.

I smile and say, "Thank you" and follow him into the house.

It's indeed a massive house and measuring the whole thing up is gonna be one hell of a task. I look around and I cannot comprehend why the guy, our client Mr. Sahota, wants to re-do the whole place. It's got a very distinct, old Punjabi *haveli* kind of style and I simply love it – high roofs, arched openings for doors and windows, nice antique panel doors with old style chain latches.

We are taken to what looks like the drawing room where the furniture is totally royal. I am looking around, observing everything in the room when Mr. Sahota says,

"Please have a seat."

I turn to him and say with a smile,

"Thank you."

"What would you like to have? Tea, coffee or some cold drink?"

"Nothing for me, thank you," I say politely.

"I would like tea please." The contractor who is sitting on the next sofa butts in.

I feel a slight tug of awkwardness at his instant greedy reaction but quickly kill my own qualms.

"Sure," Mr. Sahota says and asks me again, "Are you sure you don't want anything Mr. Rishabh?"

"Yes, nothing for me, thank you so much," I reply.

In less than five minutes, the contractor is noisily sipping his tea. Mr. Sahota has left us alone for the moment. I am sitting there awkwardly with nothing better to do than to look around the room again. The wall at the other end of the room has a lot of framed pictures hung on it. I get up and walk towards it.

I look at the pictures and it turns out that Mr. Sahota was a body builder. There are pictures of him in a variety of poses all over the wall. In some he is holding a trophy as people are congratulating him, in some others, his hands are on his waist as he is showing off numerous medals hanging around his neck, and finally, there are some pictures of him playing *kabaddi*.

"That was 20 years back." I am startled by Mr. Sahota's voice.

I turn around and smile, "Quite some achievements, I must say." He is now wearing formal clothes.

"Yes, I won quite a few championships. I made it to the nationals too." I see intense pride in his eyes.

"That is a big *achievement* sir. And you are so... senior"* God! He is talking of the time when I was five years old! I could barely speak then and would always keep crying for Uncle Chips** as I could never have enough of them!

"Thank you," he says as he continues, "And I was quite a hunter too. There is one with a leopard, there," he says, as he points to

---

* Please note that I don't want to use the word 'old' in front of him.
** A popular brand of potato wafers available when I was a kid. Highly addictive.

the row of pictures at the top that I had not noticed before. In the picture he has a dead leopard at his feet and a huge gun mounted on his shoulder. I look at it and gulp down the instant fright that rises inside me. My eyes hop from one picture to another as I see various animals – deer, bear, wild boar, all lying dead at his feet as he holds his head high with a gun in his hand. I close my eyes and picture myself lying dead at his feet while he throws his head back and laughs. I turn around and smile awkwardly without looking at him.

"I think we should start with the work, I mean... start taking the measurements." God save me!!!

"Yes, you should start with your work now. One thing though, when you start with the designing, please keep in mind that I want a contemporary look."

"Sure sir."

After a slight pause he says, "I have to leave now, Mr. Rishabh. You please carry on. My wife, Kavita, will be around. Come, I'll introduce you to her."

He calls out her name and she replies, "Coming."

In less than 30 seconds she is in front of us.

"Hi," she says as she smiles.

"Hi." I smile back.

"Kavita, please show him around." Mr. Sahota says.

"Sure," Kavita says and looks at me.

* * *

The scary hunter, Mr. Sahota has left the house and I can breathe again. It's only now that the image of him shooting me with his huge rifle starts to fade from my mind and I notice that Mrs. Sahota – Kavita, is quite a looker. She has (medium) brown eyes, long straight hair that she has left untied. Her face is a perfect oval with lips so pink, even without lipstick. And as I secretly check her out (making sure, by the way, that she does not notice me checking her out) I see that she does not have even a speck of extra fat anywhere around her waist (or anywhere else, for that matter).

"It's a regular house," she says, "three bedrooms with attached bathrooms, a kitchen, a dining room, a drawing room, a living room, a lobby and a store on the ground floor, and three bedrooms with attached toilets and balconies on the first floor and a terrace. We don't have anything but a terrace on the second floor."

"Cool," I say.

We are in the lobby now and I can see all the three bedrooms connected to it. There is a giant circular staircase (like the ones we see in those old movies) that leads to the upper floors.

"It's a very old house. Darshan's family has been staying here for generations," Kavita says and I can't restrain myself from asking,

"Why did Mr. Sahota, I mean, Mr. Darshan, move to the UK? It appears that your family is... quite well-to-do and..." I realize that I have just said something I shouldn't have and hold my tongue.

She takes a deep breath and says, "He was so mesmerized by the glamour of foreign lands. At times I really wish we had never moved. Things would have been so different then, and so much... better." She trails off into silence.

Then she looks at me and asks, "You are quite young. What plans do you have for your life?"

This is totally inappropriate and I really wish that I am imagining it, but there is an undeniable touch of flirtation in her voice. I am shocked and I stand there silent. She is still staring at me in a way she shouldn't. Why would she do that? God! Now what should I say? I mean I am the hired architect here, I can't simply say that I don't enjoy working as an architect! That would totally shake her (our client's) belief in our firm! Oh God! What have you put me into!!! I am gonna mess up the whole situation and we are gonna lose the project and my boss will fire me! No more Mr. Self-dependant then!

"Well, I love architecture. So I know... that I am gonna establish my career in that. Yeah, that's my plan, pretty much," I say as I nod.

God! I hope I didn't stammer much! I hope I made it sound real.

Ok, there is more awkward silence now and she is simply staring at me. And I don't like it. What am I supposed to do?

"I... should start... my work now. Thank you so much for... directing me and... showing me around," I stammer.

I walk to the drawing room where the Beagle-Boy look-alike contactor is sitting on a sofa, noisily eating the biscuits that he was served with the tea.

"Sir," I call him, "Let's start measuring this place up. I can start with the internal dimensions and I guess you can take care of the external dimensions of the building."

"Sure," he says, as he walks out with his instruments and his note pad. I look around the room, trying to figure out where to start.

I only wanted to hold it in my hands

Ok, I am more or less done with all the measurements. I have covered all the floors and only the three bedrooms on the ground floor are left now. I walk to the lobby and proceed to the bedrooms. I try to open a door but it's locked. Mrs. Sahota should have the keys, I guess. I go to the lobby again to see if there is any sign of her.

I don't find her, but I see an antique dressing table placed in a corner. The frame for the mirror is lavishly carved and is golden in colour while the rest of it is white. It is certainly a magnificent piece of furniture. I march towards it hypnotized and take a closer look. It must be a genuine antique, at least 100 years old. I notice three slim drawers at the bottom of the mirror and I can't contain my curiosity to pull them out to see how smoothly they draw.

I pull open the first one; it draws quite smoothly and is empty.

I open the second one; it opens with a little difficulty and is empty too.

I try to pull out the third but it won't open. I do not give up and use both my hands and all my strength and it opens with a jerk. I peep inside and to my utter shock and disbelief, it's not empty – *it's got a gun*, like the real weapon that some people use to kill other people. I swear I have never seen an actual gun in my entire life before. I look at it wide-eyed. It looks like it's made of metal. How much would it weigh? I pick it up and realize that the size of the thing is quite misleading – it's heavier than it appears to be.

There is something about these weapons. When you hold them, they make you feel different. I instantly want to pose a bit like James Bond, with the gun in my hands, and see how I look. Maybe that is why it's here, so you can pose with it and check yourself out in the mirror. Otherwise why would someone keep a gun in a dressing table drawer? I hold the gun properly and make that iconic *007* pose and look at myself in the mirror. Hmm, not bad actually, I wish I had someone to click a photograph of me now.

Just then I hear some footsteps approaching and I frantically put the gun back in the drawer and force it to close with all my might.

"Is everything ok Rishabh?" Oh my God! It's Mrs. Kavita Sahota!

"Yes, everything is perfectly fine. What could be wrong? Nothing is wrong. I was just... checking... I mean looking at myself in the mirror," I say as I look into the mirror once again, pretend to set my hair and turn around to smile at her.

She is giving me with the same creepy look. After another awkward pause I say,

"Actually... I needed to measure the bedrooms now, and I found them locked. I was...wondering if you had the keys and if I could measure them."

She smiles at me and says, "You should have mentioned this earlier," and walks towards the bedroom like a cat.

How the scary hunter's wife throws herself at me

She walks to the door, uses her key to push it open and we both walk into the room. And then she smiles at me in the same way that Mallika Sheravat looks at her fellow actors which is more than enough to seduce them out of their senses.

"This is where Darshan and I sleep, *every night*." Her voice no longer sounds normal; it has become husky in a weird way.

"Yes ma'am, and I need to measure it," I say. Something's really wrong with her.

"You can measure everything you want, including me," she says as she glares at me, pressing herself against the wall.

"… I don't think that would be… appropriate, or… necessary for the design, unless… you want us to design… furniture that is… custom made for you to… fit in… like a… key fits in a hole." Oh my God. What am I saying, *what am I saying?* What am I supposed to do???!!! Her husband!!! The killer!!! If he gets to know about all this, he is surely gonna kill me and mount my head on the wall with marbles for eyes as a part of his grand collection!!! God! No… she is coming towards me now!

"Come on now, don't be a naughty boy," she says as she makes a baby face.

What is with her? Can't she see I am being anything but naughty? *Naughty is so not what I am thinking right now.*

"Come on now, let's get on with it," she says as she pins me against the wall, "The measurements, let's *do* them."

No, no, no! There is no way out now! *There is no escape*! I am stuck!

"Kavita" I hear someone call. Oh my God! It's Mr. Sahota! He is here!!! And this is when I die!!! Oh my God! I can't breathe! Heart attack! I am getting a heart attack! I am sure this is what it feels like! Doctor! Doctor!!

As soon as Kavita hears Mr. Sahota's voice, she pulls herself back and I can no longer feel her warm breath on my lips. I am panting heavily as she quickly begins to set her hair straight and walks to the door, "Here Sweetie, you are back early?" she says as she stands in the doorway.

"Yes, there was hardly anything to do there. So I decided to come back."

"Ok," she says as she turns back to look at me, winks and moves her lips, wanting me to read them. And she says, 'next time' and throws me a kiss.

I hate the Beagle Man!

I am done with all my work and am desperate to leave. This place is an absolute death trap. I go to the Beagle contractor and check with him to ensure that we have collected all the data we need. Now I just need to find Scary Mr. Sahota and inform him that we are leaving.

The Beagle man and I find him in the living room. He and his super unfaithful wife are sitting together reading the newspaper.

I fake a cough and they both look up.

"We are done with the work, sir. We will be leaving now," I say.

"But it's lunch time, why don't you join us for lunch?" he says.

There is no way I am staying.

"Yes, please do join us for lunch," the bad lady says.

"My Mrs. has requested you now, you have to stay, I insist," he says.

Ok, I know Mr. Sahota is a very dangerous man and I must obey him and do all he says but I still feel that it's best to leave this place as quickly as possible. Quite a lot has happened, but I am sure Mr. Sahota does not know yet, and would never be able to find out, unless I mess things up further. I am sure he has no hidden camera in his bedroom – no one is that psychotic.

"Since you are insisting so much sir, we would like to join you," the contractor butts in.

Damn the Beagle Man!

Please stand up!

We are all sitting at the dining table and my throat is aching due to the tension. I look at the table and there are all kinds of preparations – butter chicken, *mattar paneer*, mutton curry... in short, we were going to eat dead, skinned animals, who had been boiled in water or fried in oil, so that their flesh became soft to bite and easy to digest.

"The chicken is really well-cooked today, isn't it?" Mr. Sahota asks me as he smiles, chewing on the drumstick he is holding.

"Yes, it is quite well-cooked," I force myself to say, faking a smile.

"So Mr. Rishabh, how long have you been working?" he asks, trying to make conversation.

"It's been over two years, I believe," I say as I run a quick calculation in my mind.

"And what kind of projects have you been working on?"

"Quite a variety of projects — residential, commercial... schools —"

Mr. Sahota unexpectedly cuts me off and asks, "Malls? Have you worked on any mall?"

"Yes I have actually, and also on a few cinema halls."

"That is very good. We want a house just like that. We want to have a house with that style. When someone looks at the house, it should look unique, different, like a mall."

"Sure." I nod.

Suddenly he grows quiet and starts looking at his plate with unseeing eyes.

"At times I feel that we should not have shifted to England," he says.

Ok, there is something wrong with these people, if they really feel that it was a bad idea to move, they why don't they come back?

"People there are... different. They are not... *our own*. This is our land; this is where we have grown up, this is where all our memories come from. This is where we first learned to... walk. And no other land can give one that feeling."

I can see Mr. Sahota has totally gone off on a journey back in time and I really want to suggest to him that he should not try to make this beautiful heritage house look like a mall as that would butcher all his memories attached with this place, and how he should only try to restore the house, but I somehow can't gather the courage. And to be honest, I am touched by his words and unknowingly, I am staring at him. No one says anything for a moment and everyone is looking at someone (apart from the Beagle Man – he is busy eating noisily). After a quick second I realize that Mr. Sahota is looking back at me and I sense the awkwardness. I immediately go back to looking at my plate and realize that I need a *chapatti*. I look around the table and see that we are momentarily out of *chapattis*.

"We need *chapattis*, Kavita," Mr. Sahota says.

Hmm, he may be an animal terminator, but he does seem like a nice host.

"Yes, I'll get some," Kavita says and she is about to get up.

"Why are you going? Where is Chotu? I haven't seen him since morning," he says.

Hmm, so they too have a servant, named Chotu. It's such an oxymoron I tell you, all these 'Chotus' are grown ups and adults, but they will always be called Chotu.

"I don't know, he was complaining of a tummy ache in the

morning. He must be working in the kitchen right now," Kavita replies.

"Nonsense, these people always give excuses because they don't want to work," he says angrily.

That is kind of true, even I complain of a tummy ache when I don't feel like going to office – it's basic human tendency.

"Chotu," he almost yells, "get some *chapattis* here," he orders.

In less than 30 seconds a small kid of probably... 5 or 6 years of age comes out of the kitchen holding a plate. He is such a cute looking kid and so young that I doubt whether he is their servant. Or maybe he is. And they just want their children to learn household work and they are making him get used to working like that. People think differently in the villages you know. He comes over and keeps the plate very timidly on the table. This is when I notice he is barefooted. I observe him for a while and find his gestures are so not what I would expect from the kid of the house.

He takes a step back and looks at Mr. Sahota.

"What happened?" Mr. Sahota asks in a very commanding voice.

"Tummy is paining Sir," he says, and it looks like he is on the verge of crying.

"Tummy is paining," Mr. Sahota mimics him, "If I give you a tight punch it will vanish." He thunders, "Now go back and work."

Ok, he is for sure no son of theirs. They have employed almost an infant to work, as a servant. *And this is not right!*

Suddenly the whole incident of the kid in the shop below my office takes over my mind and Natasha's words start ringing in my ears – *You are a big hypocrite, you always talk about working for a cause and never do anything when you get a chance.*

This is it – this is my chance. This is the time when I must stand up for the cause. Even if it puts my life at a huge risk – I know there is a gun in the house, but I must not be afraid.

I sit up straight, take a deep breath, look directly at Mr. Sahota, and prepare myself to speak up.

* * *

But wait a minute, I can't just sit and talk! I need to make this more... impactful*. I must, stand up like a total... revolutionist, and fearlessly find the right words to say. I stand up but something touches something else, and gets stuck somewhere, and the plate from which I was eating crashes to the ground with a terrible sound and there is dead silence in the room with everyone staring at me.

!!! What do I do now? This is really rude, and in no way had I meant to be rude.

"Sorry about that," I start with a firm voice, "I didn't want to break that, and be... rude." I look down at the husband and the wife. "But there is no way you can make that kid work for you as a servant like that!"

Mr. Sahota is looking at me and he does not look pleased. But I couldn't care less. It's not at all acceptable – what he is doing.

"Calm down Mr. Rishabh, we treat him like our own kid,"

---

* I am not sure if that is a word, but that is what I want my action to be.

Mr. Sahota says.

"Yeah, I can *see* that!" I shoot back.

On second thoughts, maybe he would indeed behave with his own kid too in the same way. But that does not make any difference; he has no right to behave with anyone else's kid like that.

"We even send him to school," he adds.

"Yeah? I am so sure you don't." I don't even know where this comes from, but I say it with full certainty.

"No, we really do, I mean, he is not going to school at present, but I have made all the arrangements for his admission in a good school here," he repeats.

Ok, this is irritating now. I don't even want to listen to what he is saying. Why would he lie like this? Clearly he has no such plans! I just want to call Chotu here and clarify.

"Chotu," I call out. And the kid appears in a matter of seconds. He looks confused and scared.

"Do you go to school?" I ask him.

He stands there silent, slowing shaking his head.

"Now what do you have to say?" I question them sharply.

"He does not understand what you are saying –"

I cut Mr. Sahota as he starts to speak and say, "Mr. Sahota, you don't know who you are dealing with here. I have connections with a lot of NGOs who work for this cause."

Ok, I have no such connections, but I still say that. And I have a feeling that Natasha would surely have some contacts. In any case, I don't see any harm right now in scaring him a little.

"And I know *quite a few* journalists who would be more than happy to cover this story and throw this case open to the public."

Ok, I know only one journalist, but that one journalist, according to me, is equal to a whole army of journalists.

Now the husband, the wife and the Beagle Man (who has stopped eating, by the way) are all gaping at me shocked. And I have run out of things to say.

Kid in the house

"Are you out of your mind? Do you even *have* a mind?" my Mom is totally flipping. She is pacing up and down the room and is completely out of control.

"You do not bring home... other people's kids like this!" she says as she crashes on a chair. "God! What is wrong with my son! What have you done to him? He was alright, he was alright when I gave birth to him!" she says, throwing in all the drama.

Wait, you guys don't know what has happened, let me just quickly fill you in. After that huge row I had at that huge house (Mr. Sahota's) I decided not to leave the kid there as I felt he would not be safe there. I kept imagining Mr. Sahota branding the kid's skin with a hot iron stamp that said 'Sahota's servant' as the poor kid screamed and struggled to free himself and Mr. Sahota threw his head back and gave out the most devilish laugh. So I decided to bring the kid home. It seemed to be the best thing to do at that time. Moreover this is what one is supposed to do, right? Make sure the kid is safe and then send him back to his village? That is what Savaray did, and that is what worked best at that time.

"I really don't understand what is wrong with you. First you bring a puppy home. And *now*? You brought a living human child home! This is really outrageous!" Mom rants.

"What did you want me to do? Bring a dead human child home?" I whisper, hoping she wouldn't hear what I said.

"Quiet! Don't you say another word!" she thunders.

* * *

Rishabh: i seriously don't understand what is wrong with the world we live in.

Natasha: ?

Rishabh: i told you about the kid i brought home, right?

Natasha: ya.

Rishabh: mom is making such a big issue out of it! i mean... the kid was in need, i had to bring him with me. she says that if I won't go and hand the kid over to the police, she will do it herself.

Natasha: hmm

Rishabh: you know, she didn't make this big a deal out of things when i got gabru chotta kutta young home. i mean, this is like... completely outrageous, we would accept a dog's baby and help him, but we won't help a human kid... it's really frustrating.

Natasha: i can kind of understand that.

Rishabh: ? what are you saying?

Natasha: see, you have to look at it objectively. no one can come later to claim a stray puppy. neither can anyone press charges against you for doing so. but when it comes to a human child, it comes with a lot of laws and legalities attached. anyway, chuck it. but what's your plan now? what are you gonna do with the kid?

Rishabh: see, i am definitely not handing the kid over to the police, i can't just put him in their hands, i don't trust them. i am planning to contact his parents and then i'll see how to arrange for him to go back to his village.

Natasha: hmm. good plan.

* * *

There is something about mornings that I really like. It's a fresh, brand new beginning. And the lovely golden light that pours into the house announcing the new day has something magical about it for sure. The long, sharp shadows, the chirping of the birds, and the way everything starts to stir – the lazy roads waking up again, getting ready to bear the load once again, the milkman on his way… it's all so refreshing.

I walk out to the main gate to collect the newspaper – yes, I am the first to get up today. I take the newspaper to the dining room and I sit down to read it. But just like every other day, there is nothing good in the newspaper that catches my attention. So I quickly go to the entertainment section to check what all movies are showing on TV today and to check whether there is any that I have not seen before. It's no surprise – to find no new movie in the listings. I fold the paper and get up to leave.

This is when I notice him – the boy whom I brought back from that villain's place yesterday. He is lying curled up in a corner on a mat. Morning light from the window falls on him and he has the most peaceful expression on his face as he sleeps. There is something about the whole picture that draws me towards him. I go and kneel next to him. He is sleeping like an angel and there is such innocence surrounding his whole form. The innocence that always gets washed away as one grows up. He should be enjoying his childhood. But he has been forced to work and serve people, when they should be taking care of him – serving him. I really want to do something for him; to make things better for him. I almost feel a strong urge to adopt him. And why can't I? I would definitely be able to provide a better living for him than his parents can. I am sure they are *not* well off. And everything happens for a reason, no? Maybe I came across this kid because I am supposed to adopt him – God wants me to do that – that is why God sent me there to that house to take those stupid measurements.

As I stand there looking at the sleeping child he somehow senses my presence and starts to move.

He opens his eyes slowly and looks at me. Neither of us says anything and he begins to look uncomfortable.

Finally he speaks,

"I will make tea for you, I will make breakfast."

God! He is simply tuned to talk like that. He thinks that I have brought him to my place to make him work. This is *terrible*. I look at the kid and he is so... young, so delicate. I can now understand why children are compared to flowers all the time. And what kind of person would ill-treat such a kid and scream at him? That evil Mr. Sahota! Such a person is no human, he is a monster.

This is a little kid, with his whole life in front of him. I look at him and I don't see how I was any different when I was a kid (apart from the shabby attire that is). The only difference that I can think of is that I had the resources and he doesn't have them. I was fortunate enough to go to a good school and college and get good exposure and that's it. Who knows if he has a higher IQ and can do much better in life than me?

This is when I realize that I know him only as Chotu and clearly that cannot be his real name. And I can't call him that – it's quite disrespectful. He is a human being with a proper name and I must call him by that.

"What's your name?"

"Chotu," he says, most innocently.

His simple answer brings a smile to my face.

"What's your real name? I mean, what did your Maa and Baba call you?"

"Ramesh," he says in a firm but polite voice.

"Do you want to study Ramesh? Do you want to go to school?"

He nods gently with his eyes fixed on me.

Must meet Mansi!

Mom has just stormed into the room and is looking totally out of control.

"Why is the kid still here? When is he moving out? How are you going to send him back?" she shoots the same volley of questions at me for the nth time since yesterday.

I quietly sit there sipping milk. There is a terrible awkwardness in the room as no one says anything for a moment. I look at Ramesh who is sitting huddled in a corner. There is a hole in his shirt near the shoulder, his hair looks as if it has not been washed in ages and the things that he is wearing on his feet hardly qualify as slippers – they are so worn out and tattered.

"You are not gonna do anything about it, are you?" Mom shoots again.

I still remain silent.

"Do you realize this is a real kid we have here? Do you know what kind of trouble we can get into?"

Silence.

"Give me his parents' phone number," she says.

Doesn't she realize I am not gonna do any such thing? Why can't she just get over it? The kid is gonna stay in this house for a while and the quicker she comes to terms with it, the better.

"Give me his parents' phone number Rishabh or I am gonna hand the kid to the police." She glares at me.

Oh my God, she is fuming! She looks totally capable of doing what she just said! I instantly take out the chit of paper on which I had written Ramesh's parents' phone number yesterday and keep it on the table in front of her.

"Here, take it. And stop calling him 'the kid,' he has a name, Ramesh."

She looks even angrier now as she takes the piece of paper with her eyes fixed on me.

She dials the number from her cell phone and says,

"Can I talk to Ramesh's parents please?"

She holds on for a moment and then again speaks into the phone, "Namaste, your son, Ramesh is with us. We found out that some people were keeping him in their house and was making him work for them. We just felt that it would be best if we sent him back to you."

After this she is quiet for a while, like for a minute or even longer. Then she finally speaks up,

"I am sorry to have troubled you." And she hangs up.

She is marching out of the room when I anxiously ask her, "What happened?"

Without turning back, she replies, extremely irritated, "Forget the parents; the kid is staying with us."

!!!

* * *

Rishabh: supposedly the parents were not happy that we got the kid with us as he was to send them money.

Natasha: hmm

Rishabh: and mom was particularly furious when they started accusing her and went ranting about what a huge problem she had created for them and said 'you rich people can never understand our problems'.

Natasha: hmm

Rishabh: supposedly they have like some six kids and all of them work. ramesh is the youngest.

Natahsa: hmm. so the kid, i mean ramesh is gonna stay with you guys now.

Rishabh: yes!

Natasha: so what's the plan now?

Rishabh: well, since i met mansi a few days back and she is a teacher, i am gonna meet her and ask her for tips that i can use when i start teaching ramesh (yes, i am gonna home school him.)

Natasha: so you are gonna meet mansi?

Rishabh: yes.

Natasha: and ask her for tips for teaching.

Rishabh: yes.

Natasha: good ☺ *ek teer se do nishane.*

Rishabh: :P

* * *

It's hard to believe, but it's true – yes, I am late to meet Mansi and Janvi. I was supposed to reach the coffee shop at 7 and it's 7:15 already. Something is really wrong with me and I don't know when I am gonna improve – when I will learn to be on time!

I push the glass door of the coffee shop open and look around. The place is buzzing with people but there is no sign of either Mansi or Janvi.

With luck I find a table for three vacant and occupy it instantly. It takes me around 15 seconds to decide that I want to listen to some music on my phone as I wait. No, wait, maybe I should read a book. Girls find that more impressive, yes I should do that. But what books am I carrying with me? Let me see, I have *The Best of Maupassant* – pass, *The Best of Mulk Raj Anand* – pass, *Veronica Decides To Die* – pass (I don't want to die), *David Copperfield* – yes! This is it! This is what I am gonna read! Girls dig classics, I know. Last time I didn't get a chance to flaunt my reading habit. This time I am not gonna miss it. And this one is my favourite too. I can talk for hours if she wants to discuss the book with me. I pull the book out and open it when I hear someone say,

"Hi!" It's Janvi.

"Hey! Hi, I didn't... see you guys coming," I stammer as they have come at a completely unexpected moment.

"What book are you reading?" Janvi asks. And she is looking at the book with such anticipation that if I don't hand over the book to her, she is gonna snatch it from my hands.

"It's *David Copperfield*, one of my all time favourites."

"Uh! Classics, how boring, I am reading *Twilight* these days and am totally in love with it. You should read it too, it's really cool. The vampires and the werewolves are simply awesome I tell you. I wish I could find one for myself, they are so... *hot*!" she says as she sits down and I see that Mansi is still standing. Ok, I have really bad manners, I have completely lost all my chivalry; a girl is standing in front of me and I have not even offered her a seat. I immediately stand up and say,

"Please sit down," with a smile.

She smiles back and sits down. She is wearing a gentle pinkish white *salwar* suit and is looking like a total angel.

"But Mansi is a total sucker for classics; she likes everything that is boring," Janvi adds.

See, I told you, girls like classics.

"I just love this book. And I think everyone can relate to the story at one level or the other," I say, looking at Mansi.

"That is very true." Mansi smiles back.

"Please don't start discussing the book now, please! So, Rishabh, tell us, the kid you were talking about, the one that you kidnapped. What about him?" Janvi says.

I look at her and say, "One, I didn't kidnap him, I rescued him. And two, please don't call him the kid ever again, his name is Ramesh." I am irritated.

"Wow, *ok*, please don't strangle me to death for that – it's the kid, not Ramesh," she says and instantly corrects herself, "I mean, it's *Ramesh*, and not the kid. God! How touchy you are!"

"Thank you," I say politely.

"It's ok, now would you please tell us why you called us? I don't have all evening here you know?" Janvi says.

"Yes I know that. And I don't intend to keep you all evening here either –" I say, when Janvi cuts me off again.

"Yeah, right. So would you please get on with it already?"

Ok, this girl really knows how to irritate me. I clear my throat, look at Mansi and say, "I found Ramesh at my client's house where they were making him work as their servant. I took him home with me and contacted his parents and tried to send him back. But it turned out that they don't want him back as they wanted him to earn money and send it to them. I just happened to ask this kid… I mean Ramesh," I pause to look at Janvi, who is already staring at me, catching the slip of my tongue, "whether he wanted to study, and he said yes, so I thought that since you are a teacher, you could give me useful tips that I can use while I teach Ramesh." I look back at Mansi.

"God! You are a total nutter!" Janvi says with a sigh.

I completely ignore her and say, "And do you know we have hunters living around us? Like real hunters who have guns, who go kill live animals?"

A for Apol

It was a great meeting with Mansi, (and Janvi) she gave me quite a few helpful tips and when we were all leaving, I said that if I needed any more help from her, I would call her and she smiled and said 'sure' which totally made my day. So here I am sitting with Ramesh and we are gonna start the class now. I know now that children can remember things better if we help them associate words with images and sounds. So I have got a few charts and books to help Ramesh register things better. They are nice, bright and colourful. I feel even adults would like them, I myself think they are quite nice. And we are gonna start with English. And that is only fair, no? Because back in school, the first period always was the English period. It would be fun though, to ask him to draw things, like animals and objects. But I feel we should get down to some serious business first. I am going to start with alphabets. I spread the chart on the table and say,

"Now speak after me, 'A...'"

"A" he says.

"A for apple."

"A for apol," he says.

"No, no. It's not A for apol, it's A for apple," I repeat.

"A for apol," he repeats. I look at him as he is looking at me with his big, hopeful and eager eyes. I am completely clueless as to how to explain to him that it's not 'apol', but 'apple'. Hmm, maybe I should take this up later and just move on to the next alphabet for now.

I move my finger to the next alphabet 'B' and say it out loud.

"V" he says.

"No, no, it's not 'V', it's 'B'. 'B' for boy," I say as I point to the picture of the boy on the chart.

Ramesh has a huge grin on his face now and is saying, "V for Voy."

Then he puts his finger on the picture of the boy and repeats with a joyful little laugh, "Voy. Ha ha." And then he puts his hand on his chest and repeats again, "Voy".

Well, the kid is smart. He has understood the basic concept –

what 'boy' means. But he needs to pronounce it correctly.

"Ramesh, it's not 'voy', it's, boy. It's 'B', like, *ba*, as in *bahar*'."

"*Ba, bahar,*" he repeats after me.

!!! See! I told you he would get it soon enough!

"Yes! Good boy! Now repeat after me, 'B for boy'."

"V for voy."

Ok, I need some professional help here. I don't know how to correct him.

"Voy." He is looking at me and there is a distinct shine of achievement in his eyes.

"Boy," I say disappointed.

"Kaku also wants to study," he suddenly says.

Who is Kaku? Must be his imaginary friend. Hmm, no big deal, I have heard children make imaginary friends all the time. So he just wants me to teach his imaginary friend as I teach him. That's totally doable. No! Wait a minute, this is not as simple as it looks. It is very much possible that it's not a simple case of an imaginary friend, but a very serious case of schizophrenia! Oh my God he is a nutcase! He is gonna come in the middle of the night sometime when I am sleeping, with a huge knife in his hand, just like they showed in those evil doll *'Chucky'* movies, and *kill me*!

No, no. Wait. I must calm down. He is not a nutcase, *I* am – I must stop freaking out like this. There is nothing wrong with this kid and I just need to figure out who Kaku is. I simply ask him,

"Who is Kaku?"

"My friend. He lived in our village. He also came to the city with me. He works in the house next to the house where I worked."

Hmm. Now I certainly can't go and bring Kaku from the house next to Mr. Sahota's, definitely not this soon – I created quite a scene there only days ago.

* * *

I have just reached office *but I don't feel like working*. Actually I didn't feel like coming to office today, but one must do what one has to. I feel restless and for some reason I feel like having Pepsi. It helps you know, it gives you a kick start and instant energy. It's a different thing that it has like loads and loads of calories which make you fat and some people even claim that it dissolves your bones, but today I don't care about any of it. I call for Savaray, give him a 50 rupee note and ask him to get a 500 ml bottle of Pepsi for me.

"I will finish cleaning up and then go," he says and then laughs like a five year old kid, showing as many teeth as he possibly could.

Now who would not feel awkward seeing such a gesture?

But I look back at him blankly and say, "Ok."

For some unknown reason, I feel unsettled today. Is it the office environment or the fact that I am the only employee here (apart from the peon), I don't know.

"It's a really sad office, anyone would go mad working here," I say.

"You and I are 50 percent mad," he says blankly.

I know I need to start working now but I just can't recall what I was working on. It takes me a full three minutes to remember that I was preparing a drawing of Mr. Sahota's house using the measurements we took that day. Ugh! The mere thought of him gives me the creeps. Such a terrible person! I mean who goes around killing animals and employing infants as servants. Ok, fine, maybe Ramesh is not an infant, but he is still a small child and he should not be made to work. He should be free to do whatever he likes, to explore things... to enjoy his childhood.

Anyway, I need to get my mind off this – I am in office and I must follow office decorum – must work. I spread the sheet on the drafting table, adjust and align it with the T-square, fix it in place with tape, pick up the set-square and the pen and begin drafting. I have barely drawn three lines when Savaray comes into the studio grinning and says,

"You know, it's Diwali today."

Ok, now this confirms that something is wrong with him today. I know it's not true for two distinct reasons. One – it's a working day at the office today, and two – *it's not Diwali season yet.*

"What?"

"Yes it *is*. See, someone gave me *50 rupees*."

"Savaray, I gave you the money to get Pepsi for me. Now please don't irritate me and just get what I asked you to."

He goes to the window and says,

"See, donkeys," as he points outside.

I do not reply.

He turns around and asks, "Have you ever ridden a donkey?"

"No Savaray." I don't even know why I reply.

"I have," he says laughing as he nods vigorously.

"Back in my village, we have so many donkeys. And when we have to go long distances, like from one village to another, we ride on donkeys," he continues.

His words compel me to imagine him sitting on a donkey. And the picture that appears in my mind is nice. From the expression on the donkey's face to the expression on his face to the whole landscape, everything looks really peaceful and joyous.

"It must be really nice to stay in a village, isn't it?" I say, and cannot resist a smile.

"It is!" he says, vigorously nodding his head again as he walks towards me. "We have so much fun there. Such vast fields, streams, trees! It's very good."

Now I am thinking about Ramesh again. How he too must belong to such a place. And I realize that there is hardly anyone with whom I can share all that has been happening lately. Thoughts are bubbling inside my head, demanding to be told.

"You know, I got this kid from one of our clients. And I was trying to teach him how to read and write and he told me there was a friend of his who also wanted to study. Now I could not find that kid, but I went searching in all the houses around my house and I found quite a few children working as servants," I say.

"People who make small children work should be shot in public!" he says sternly.

"Shut up. So I went to those houses and talked to the owners. I told them that I was a volunteer for an NGO that works for the well being of underprivileged kids and we have a program to teach these kids."

"But you don't work for an NGO, you work for Sir," he interrupts.

"I know, I just made that up. But that's not important, and will you please just listen to me?" I reply, irritated.

"Ok, then?"

"So I told them that they should send the kids to attend the morning class that I will be holding and if they didn't do that, I would escalate the matter to the police."

"Then?"

"Then what? They agreed."

"Yaee!"

"I know. And I will be conducting these classes with the help of a school teacher I met a few days back. I am really excited about it."

"Is this a girl teacher?" he asks.

"Yes."

"You *like* that girl."

"Shut up, there is nothing like that."

Then he actually starts jumping and says, "You know, Manju and I, we had so much fun last night."

"God! Savaray, please don't start again."

Let things begin

It's early morning and I am in a park. I have not come here just for fun, I am here for some serious business. After I went looking for children in the neighbourhood, I was able to gather a total of 11 children. Mansi, Janvi and I decided to pool in some money and buy some basic stationery and teaching aids. We put together a few things in a carton – some very nice notebooks (which have pictures from the super cool Disney movie *'Up'* on the cover), some books about basic stuff like alphabets and numbers and some pencils. Other than that, there are some charts and a very nice portable blackboard.

It's a huge park. Actually, it's not like a *park* kind of park, it's a huge piece of land covered with grass, flanked by a row of trees on one side. And it's the best and most beautiful setting I could think of, near my house, to teach the children. As a kid I used to come here to play cricket with my friends. And every time we came here to play, I would be the one who had to bring along a ball from home and the ball would always get lost somewhere. Now if I think about it, this place has something... uncanny about it – it eats cricket balls. I hope it does not eat kids; because then I would be in *big* trouble. Or maybe the place didn't eat cricket balls. Maybe my friends hid the balls and gave the lame excuse that they couldn't find it so that they could take them home later. Hmm, so I've been a fool since childhood. But anyway, I don't need to think about it now – I no longer care for those stupid, childish playthings.

I sit down on the grass and simply look around. Everything is so fresh and beautiful. The sky is a clear blue, a cool wind is blowing and birds are flying from one tree to another. I can feel peace everywhere. Closing my eyes, I take a deep breath and feel vitally refreshed.

Ramesh is sitting next to me and he does not move his eyes away from the book that I have given him for even an instant.

I notice two girls walking in my direction. Mansi and Janvi. Mansi is wearing a beautiful white *salwar* suit and the cool breeze is playing with her hair that she has left untied.

She comes and stands in front of me and I say, "You look beautiful," as I smile.

"Thank you", she says with a smile looking back at me.

"Ahem." It's Janvi. I look at her and she says,

"Some people aren't invisible you know," she says.

I turn to her and say, "I am so sorry. You look really good too." Actually I don't even notice what she is wearing and how she looks – I just say it anyway.

"Yeah, *yeah*."

I turn to Mansi and say, "The kids should be here any minute now. They are... expected to be here like... any moment."

"Ok," she says.

"We can all sit for a while probably until they get here. Or... maybe not. Your white suit... it would get dirty with green stains from the grass. So we shouldn't sit. But maybe, if I had some spare old... newspaper with me, then you could have spread that on the ground and sat on it. But I don't remember getting any newspapers –"

"Oh, cut it out already," Janvi interrupts, "She is not as big a freak as you, she can sit on grass. Mansi just sit *yaar*."

Mansi smiles at me and sits down.

I am still standing, not knowing how to hide my embarrassment over my awkward blabbering.

"Now do you need a special formal request to sit down?" Janvi looks at me angrily.

"No, not at all." I let out a pretentious laugh. And sit down.

* * *

Alright, so it turns out that I am as terrible at dealing with kids as I am at teaching them. Actually, I can handle kids like one at a time. But when it comes to handling a group of children, it's different. And among the three of us, Janvi is the best at it. She raises her voice when required and is totally natural about it. And the kids are really listening to her too. And Mansi is great with them as well – she is helping them write – you know, how you hold the hand and make them write so that they learn and write without help later. I am the only one who isn't doing much and am standing, leaning against a tree. Mansi looks gorgeous, she is so... beautiful and... delicate and her *dupatta* is lightly fluttering in the breeze. It's so nice – the whole situation. I suddenly feel that I am in that Shah Rukh movie, the one in which he goes to a village and brings about a revolution. *Swades* it was called, right?

I feel a soft pat on my leg and look down. It is Ramesh. He has a big notebook in his hands, which he is finding difficult to hold, and wants to show me something in it.

I kneel down and smile, "Have you written something?"

He nods happily with a humongous sense of achievement. He points to his notebook and says, "Boy." And then he puts his hand on his chest and says, "*Mai bhi*, boy."

"*Hey*! This is really good. You are a very good boy. *Very good*," I say as I hug him and kiss him on the forehead. Ok, this is really overwhelming for me and I almost can't hold back my emotions. Mansi is really great at this. I tried for 3 complete hours and couldn't do it and she does it in less than 20 minutes. I look at Mansi to find that she is looking intently at me and is now smiling. I smile back at her and she goes to the next kid and helps him write.

Now this is when I feel like singing a song. You know, like they do in the movies when the hero dances around the heroine for whom he has become absolutely invisible and she can't even hear him. But since this is a book, you are not gonna be able to hear me sing, so please feel free to imagine me singing your favourite love song as I dance around Mansi; and just like me, you too enjoy the moment.

* * *

Natasha: so, other than falling like head over heels for mansi, what else did you do during today's class?

Rishabh: excuse me, i did not fall head over heels for mansi.

Natasha: hello? who wanted to sing songs dancing around her?

Rishabh: that is… because… i am dramatic in some ways.

Natasha: ? who are you kidding? and anyway, it's ok even if you did. coz she sounds like a nice girl.

Rishabh: i am not falling for her.

Natasha: anyway. tell me, how did the class actually go?

Rishabh: went quite well actually. the kids are responding well.

Natasha: good.

Rishabh: but we need to work on the kids, there are some basic hygiene issues. like none of them use a handkerchief. and if they have a running nose, they simply use their shirt sleeves or something. one kid actually used mansi's *dupatta* to blow her nose without even asking her. we need to teach them to develop a habit of carrying a handkerchief first of all. and then teach them to have a bath regularly, especially wash their hair and apply oil. i have a strong feeling that some of them have lice in their hair.

Natahsa: why? did you catch some?

Rishabh: no :/

Natasha: haha. but jokes apart – it's a really nice effort you guys are putting in. this is actually something about which i can say that i am proud of you.

Rishabh: thank you ☺.

Natasha: and I want to bring this effort to notice. we might just inspire some other people to do things like these.

Rishabh: yes, that would be cool.

Natasha: you know something, i am getting a few days off from work. maybe i can come down to your town myself and see how you guys conduct the class and then i can push the story to the papers.

Rishabh: wow! that would be really cool!

Natasha: i know ☺

Rishabh: ☺

Natasha: how's work going by the way?

Rishabh: it's going well. the usual. only that… things really need to be upgraded there. i mean for heaven's sake, who drafts by hand these days? but anyway, i am over the whole thing now. i just go there to work and earn money. so it's fine.

Natasha: good.

Rishabh: but there is one thing that's weird. you remember that caretaker at the office i told you about, right?

Natasha: yes, what about him?

Rishabh: it's just that he and his wife, they just keep having sex like every other day. it's like they don't have anything else to do.

Natasha: ya, i know. that's one of the major problems with that section of the society. the low literacy rate and lack of sources of entertainment kind of drive them to that.

Rishabh: ya.

Natasha: anyway, i got to go now, have loads of work to finish. catch u later.

Rishabh: k bye.

Natasha: and i am seriously gonna try and cover your story.

Rishabh: thnx.

Natasha: gn. bye.

Rishabh: bye ☺

What does he know about design?

It's a big day today – major meeting scheduled for the day with Mr. Sahota. As per the (Boss') report, Mr. Sahota has decided to put behind him the whole thing that happened at the house, and go ahead with the project. And yes, I think that is actually the only reason my boss has not fired me after the huge scolding the other day. We are to have a design discussion and hopefully freeze a concept and start developing the design. I have been working on the design for a week now and have come up with five; yes you read it right – *five* different concepts. Right now I am preparing the final sheets. I have colour pencils scattered all around me and am colouring the sheets like a maniac. So much so that my hand has started to ache. I look around for Savaray and ask him to get tea for me.

In less than two minutes he brings me a steaming cup of tea.

I sit down away from the drafting board, sipping the tea.

"So, how's everything at home?" I ask Savaray.

"Everything is good," he replies and then after a short pause and a bubbly giggle he says, "You know, the other day Manju had a dream. She saw that we both were… having fun and Sir was standing at the door watching us."

"God! Do you guys ever think of anything else?"

"He he he, no!" he grins.

"God!"

"And then we see Sir standing there but we still don't stop. And then Sir says, 'you are living in a city, not in a village. You must not do it front to front. You should do it back to front or else you will have so many children you won't be able to handle it.'"

"Savaray, you really should shut up."

"But you know, I think there is a problem. Manju's cycle isn't on time this month," he continues.

The only way Savaray might just stop talking about all this is if I don't reply. So I must not utter a word.

Just then Sir rings the bell which is a signal to call Savaray and I give out a sigh of relief.

He comes back in less than a minute and says, "Sir is calling you."

* * *

I have lost all doubts about it now – Mr. Sahota is the worst client ever. I have presented all five of the concepts in front of him and he has rejected *all of them*. He didn't like any of them, not even the one in which I suggested the magnanimous dome made of glass with spectacular stained glass paintings on it, inspired by the Mysore Palace. I really don't understand why he does not like it. It is one of the best features I have ever designed. The mere thought of sunlight entering through that dome and lighting up the whole space with those beautiful subtle hues makes my skin break into gooseflesh. And just imagine the beautiful patterns it would cast on the floor which are gonna change constantly throughout the day. It would be like the design is alive! Even Sir loved the idea and was absolutely supportive about it. But Mr. Sahota doesn't like it. He looks at the drawing and shakes his head disapproving the idea like a five year old kid who wants to eat nothing but chocolate and would under no circumstances take even a morsel of the vegetable that has been prepared for dinner. If nothing else he should at least respect the amount of time and hard work I have put in, to prepare the stunningly beautiful drawings.

"Sir, these designs are not what I am looking for," Mr. Sahota says, his words followed by silence.

Then he turns to me and says, "You worked on the concepts?"

"Yes," I say boldly.

Then he turns back to Sir and says, "These days these children don't have full knowledge about design. They come fresh out of college and think they know everything. Sir I request you to take a personal interest in this project."

??? How can he say that? What does he think of himself?! And he is saying I don't have any knowledge about design? I can give him lectures on design principles for a full week, non-stop and still have loads left over. On the contrary, what does he know about it? I am sure he knows zilch about design.

Sir stares at me and he does not look very happy. Then he clears his throat, smiles and speaks, "Mr. Sahota, I assure you that our team here is adequately professionally qualified to work on your project. And I did take full personal interest in your project; I give complete attention to all the projects that we take up in this office. However, if these design concepts are not to your taste, we will rework them and have another presentation for you."

Mr. Sahota looks at me again with actual blood shot eyes as if I am his age-old enemy and I find the anger in his eyes hard to believe. Then he looks back at Sir and asks, "When can we have the next presentation?"

Ok, it's official now – I hate Mr. Sahota. (And yes, I know hate is a strong word.)

She actually came!

It's a super-exciting day today – Natasha is here. I went to pick her up at the railway station, early in the morning and dropped her at her hotel. I really wanted her to stay at my place but she said that it would be uncomfortable for her. That made no sense to me whatsoever, but you know, there is no point arguing with Natasha – you can never force her.

Anyway, we are at the park now – our official class space, and all set to go. Everyone is here. Natasha is standing next to a tree and is speaking something into her voice recorder. I look at her and smile. She smiles back. She is looking different today. She is wearing a nice colourful kurta and a pair of deep blue jeans. She does not look one bit like the Natasha I met at the party. Which, now if I think about it, was the only time that I had seen her before today, actually.

"So it's addition and subtraction today, right?"

It's Mansi, she is talking about what we are to teach the children today.

"Yes, that's the programme for today," I say with total zest.

"Let's start with it then," she says and we both turn to face the kids to begin the class.

* * *

Class was wonderful today. The children were so well behaved and I am sure Natasha is gonna write a great story about all of this. The children have gone back; I am packing up and Natasha, Mansi and Janvi have been talking for over 15 minutes now, that's like a quarter of an hour!

I am still gathering our things when I see Mansi coming towards me.

"You need any help with this?" she asks.

"No, it's almost done," I smile.

"Ok then, Janvi and I are leaving. See you tomorrow."

"Hey wait! What did you think of Natasha?" I ask. I am really curious to know how they got along. It's very important that she gets along well with my friends.

"She is a really nice person," she says as she takes a little pause and continues, "I didn't know you were such intense friends."

She only uses the term 'intense friends' but I sense an intense undertone of 'something else.'

"See you tomorrow," she says. And then she leaves.

I pick up the carton and walk over to Natasha.

"So, how was it?" I ask.

"It was quite nice actually, I didn't know you could be so…"

"Confident?" I put in.

"Not quite the word I was looking for, but yeah, you can say that."
She smiles.

"I don't know, these kids and us, we have just somehow
established a connection. And during the class, everything
happens so naturally. I don't even have to put in any effort. My
behaviour surprises me actually, at times.

It's… funny and… weird in some ways."

"I think it's brilliant," she says as she looks right into my eyes, "I
think it's something that you were pulled here for."

I smile and say, "Possible, now tell me, what are you doing for the
rest of the day? You are going back by the evening train, right?"

"Well, I have no plans, apart from catching the train in the
evening," she says, laughing.

"Great!" I say, "Then let me just call in sick and give my boss a
heart attack. We must spend this day together."

New dynamics

It's the best day I have had in the longest time; we have been
driving all over town and I have been showing her all the
interesting places around. I showed her the play school I went to,
the primary school I went to, the hospital I was born in; all the
places.

What? It's not my fault. There is no interesting place here – apart from the ones that have memories attached.

Now we are sitting in my favourite restaurant waiting for our food to arrive. It's funny in some ways – I have so many 'friends' in this town, whom I have grown up with, and I connect to none of them and there is this one person whom I have known not even for a year and I can share almost everything with her.

"So Mansi, hmm? Nice girl she is, I like her," Natasha says.

"Yes, I like her too," I say most obviously.

"And I think she likes you too."

"Really? Did she say anything about me?" I jump.

"Well…" She trails off into silence as she rolls her eyes naughtily.

"Oh please Natasha! Don't do this. Just tell me what she said."

"Ahum, so easily?"

"What do you want me to? WHAT DO YOU WANT ME TO DO?"

"Well…"

"Aaaaaa! Natasha, please!"

"Ok, ok chill. She didn't particularly *say* anything I just sensed it from… the way she talked about you, that you are really caring, and how your heart is really pure and people as genuine as you are really rare."

"Really, she said all that?"

"Yes."

"Ah" I let out a sigh.

After a moment of silence, I ask Natasha,

"What about you? Are you gonna remain single forever?"

Silence.

"What? Say something."

She only smiles and says nothing.

"Oh, come on!" I insist.

"I think I am not the relationship type."

"Oh please, don't give me that! How can there be no one at all in your life?"

"If there were someone, don't you think I would have been in a relationship?"

"I guess…"

There is a moment of silence and she finally speaks up.

"I just feel that a relationship develops over time and the feeling is mutual. Two people need to love each other first. And if they *both* love each other, they would know, and there would be a relationship. And I don't think that has happened in my case yet, or that there is any possibility of that happening." She says this as she looks me right in the eye.

I look back at her and it's only after a few seconds that I realize that I should say something. She is so clear about everything in life.

"Wow! You *are* a writer. You know, you should not stick to like, only journalism but try your hand at other kinds of writing too – fiction maybe?" She simply smiles and looks back at me and says,

"I wonder where the food is, I am *really* hungry."

* * *

"I know, isn't she great? She is like the wisest person I know," I say. I am with Mansi at a coffee shop. Natasha had left early on in the evening and as I had taken the day off, I just thought of meeting Mansi. For some reason, she is a little quieter than usual today. I don't know what's up with her.

She keeps looking at me for a while and then finally says, "She is more than a friend, isn't she?"

"Who? Natasha? Are you kidding me? *No way*! She is *so* not the relationship type." Mansi just keeps looking at me as I say this, "And that is not what I say, that is what *she* says. So that cannot be a lie."

Mansi looks at the ground for a while before she speaks up, "It's just that... someone who is such a major part of your life needs to have an emotional attachment with you, and..."

"Hey, hey, hey, we are just friends." God! What's gotten into her today?

She looks at me and asks, "And you too never had any kind of special feelings for her?"

Ok, I should not lie to her – I was attracted to her when I first met her at the party. But things turned out to be totally different when I actually got to know her. And those were no *feelings*, it was just some basic... attraction.

"Mansi," I speak up, "We don't have that kind of a relationship, and for so many reasons. I am not her type, first of all. I am too...

goofy and... stupid for her. She's so smart and... intelligent. I can't even think about her like that. She is like my... best friend whom I turn to whenever I am in trouble. And most of all, she deserves someone way better than me." I say this as I look at a distant tree with unseeing eyes. "She deserves someone more... confident and... powerful and more... serious than me."

Mansi looks at me for a while and says, "Sounds to me more like you are saying that *you* don't deserve *her*." Really, I don't know what's wrong with Mansi today. "Mansi, it's not that kind of a relationship I have with her. It's not what you are thinking," I say looking into her eyes. How do I make her believe the truth?

"I understand," she says as she smiles.

Cause celeb

It has actually happened! She really did it!!! They have published the story in the paper!!! With pictures of us and the kids and everything! It's morning and I am in the dining room with today's newspaper in front of me. It's a full-length article, which starts like this –

City lad comes forth. If everyone was as courageous and righteous as Rishabh Suri, the world would definitely be a better place.

There is an actual, 500-word newspaper article that mentions me. God! It really feels great! People are actually gonna read this – so many people. And it's gonna be super cool when I go walking on the road and a complete stranger taps my shoulder and asks, 'Excuse me, are you Rishabh Suri – the great social activist?' And I nod my head most modestly and say 'yes'. I am gonna be a celebrity in this town and have a say in everything that happens here – I am gonna bring about great social reforms. Wow! Moving back to my home town was a fantastic idea. I am never ever gonna regret it in life!

Just then Mom enters the dining room and I jump, "Mom! See, they have featured an article that talks about our classes!"

"Really?" she swiftly comes over to me and grabs the newspaper, "Where?" she asks, and after she locates the article, she sounds super thrilled, "Hey! They even got a picture of you. And hey, look, Ramesh is there too."

I take a moment to look at the picture. It is a rather nice picture. Everyone looks very happy in the picture. There is genuine happiness in the eyes of the children. Mansi looks stunningly sophisticated and really gorgeous with a beautiful smile on her face. I am looking slightly awkward but not all that bad and Janvi is grinning showing all her teeth like a chimpanzee.

My Mom hugs me, kisses me on my forehead and says with shining eyes, "Now I can proudly brag about you with all my kitty members and tell them how proud I am of my son."

* * *

It's a day of celebration today. I just had a word with Mansi over the phone and she was equally thrilled to see the article in the paper. This whole thing has entirely lifted our spirits and we are making new plans to teach the kids better. This is so awesome and I just can't keep this thing to myself. I have already thanked Natasha like a 100 times over the phone and each time she has said 'Chill, it's cool.' I don't know how I am ever gonna pay her back.

Once in the office, I just can't wait to show the paper to Savaray.

I enter the studio and see him sitting on a chair next to the window.

"Hey, Savaray, see, there is news about me in the newspaper."

He smiles and says, "Show."

I eagerly take the paper out of my bag and show it to him.

He smiles and says, "Nice, what have they written?" he looks at me with eager eyes.

"About me and my friends, about teaching the children."

"That's a very good thing," he says.

"Yes, it is. And I want you to go to the market and get 20 copies of this newspaper for me," I say and hand him the money. I want to preserve as many copies of today's newspaper as possible. It's like the first time ever that anything has been written about me in the papers and I just... want to save as many copies as I possibly can. If it were up to me, I would buy all the copies of today's edition of the paper and stuff my whole house with it. But then, where would we stay? So I can't do that. But I can save at least 20 copies and get a few laminated to preserve them forever.

I look at Savaray and he is still sitting in the same place and I feel that his reaction is not even close to what I had expected. He keeps jumping and hopping like an excited kid all the time and today when I expected him to give a similar kind of reaction, he has gone all dull.

"What is wrong Savaray? Is everything ok?"

"Manju is pregnant."

"Hey! That is great news! Congratulations! I told you if you keep... doing that so often, there were gonna be... more of you."

"Thank you Sir," he smiles.

He does not look happy at all. Maybe he was not expecting this to happen. But it's ok, my Mom always says that if you think about such things too much then the family would never... be complete. One just has to take it as it comes and... complete one's family. He is gonna take time to come to terms with this, but I know he'll be fine in the end. And it's a great thing that he's gonna have a baby soon. Because when the baby grows up a little, we would have another student for our classes. Hopefully by that time we would have like expanded a lot and become a *huge* name.

"You are welcome," I smile back, "Now go and get the papers."

* * *

I finally get to work on the drawing when my phone starts to vibrate in my pocket. I pull it out to see an unknown number flashing on the screen. It must be one of those promotional calls again. I really find it irritating when my number gets passed on to these databases by the store owners who claim to take my number only to send me updates about *their* own new offers. I am gonna sue them all one day.

"Hello?" I take the call.

"Hello, is this Rishabh Suri?" There's a woman on the other end of the line.

"Yes… who is this?" I ask.

"This is Mrs. Simran. I used to teach you back in school, 10th standard."

Oh my God! I absolutely remember her! She used to be my favourite teacher! She threw this great party at her place, right after the formal school farewell party. And she made the most wonderful chocolate cake ever. And that icing, God! That icing on the cake had like some 10 big molten Dairy Milk chocolates in it. It was so yummy that just the mere memory of it makes my mouth water.

"Hey! Good morning Ma'am, how are you?" I say.

"I am good Rishabh, how are you?" I can almost hear her smile.

"I am good. God! It's been such a long time!"

"It sure has been a long while and I see that you have changed quite a bit."

"I don't think I have changed at all ma'am," I smile.

"Well, to take such bold steps for social upliftment, that sure speaks of a change."

"Oh Ma'am, that was nothing. It's just a small little thing that a few friends of mine and I are doing. It's just that… you know how the media blows things out of proportion these days."

"Yeah, actually you haven't changed much. You are still as humble and down to earth as you used to be."

"Oh come on Ma'am."

"Anyway, I am not gonna take much of your time, so let me straightaway get to what I called you for – congratulations for the article being featured in the paper, it's a huge thing. I am really happy to know that one of my students still has the values that I once tried to infuse. And to celebrate that, I want you to come over to my place for tea this Saturday."

"Thank you so much Ma'am. And sure, I'll definitely come."

The love song

It's marvelous weather today. We are in the park early in the morning and the sky is entirely cloudy; beautiful shades of grey is all we see. A super cool breeze is blowing and everything is just heavenly. It is such a great feeling to feel the breeze ruffling your hair like this. Nature is the best I tell you. And the class is also going really great today. All the students are well behaved. Janvi is handling the kids today and this is the reason that Mansi and I are sitting under the tree.

God just makes some people wholly perfect, doesn't He? I mean just look at her. Let's start with her hair; it's silky, long and shines, like the hair they show in all those shampoo ads. And just look at her skin – it's fair and absolutely flawless and that makes it utterly irresistible to touch. But I can't do that as we are not *that close*. She has the cutest ears; so well defined and proportionate. Her eyes are brown and if I really concentrate and look at them I can see the beautiful pattern of the iris. She has a perfect bee-stung mouth which, when she smiles, makes my heart melt.

"Do you sing?" I ask her out of the blue.

"Yeah, sometimes. But what put singing into your mind all of a sudden?"

"I don't know; they generally start singing when they have such a set up, no? Nice weather, natural setting... cool breeze..." Should I be saying this? *Should I be saying this???*

"Do you sing?" she asks me, laughing cutely.

"No; not at all, I don't, actually, I can't; I can't sing, I croak."

"Come on, it can't be that bad."

"You have no idea." I smile at her as I look into her eyes.

Silence.

"Why don't you sing a song?" I have no idea where all my manners have vanished.

"Here?"

"Yes"!!! What's wrong with me?

"Ok," she says as she laughs again, a little awkwardly this time. "What song would you like to hear?"

"The one you like the most." Ok, I should shut up right now!

She smiles, "There is this new Rahat Fateh Ali Khan song *'Mai tenu samjhva ki...'*

"Sure!" I say with enthusiasm.

She closes her eyes and starts to sing. She sings divinely. Her singing not only makes me feel as if I am floating on a cloud, but I also feel as if my heart has been set free inside my chest and is floating inside. Everything around me just becomes more beautiful – it's like one of those landscape paintings that appear to burst out of the canvas with freshness. And the song is like the most beautiful thing ever. It talks about love for someone, saying... how can I make you understand that my heart does not seek anything but your company and you would never understand my love but I will always wait for you... Mansi's voice is as beautiful as she is. She sings the song so melodiously that the song becomes even more beautiful than it already is.

She finishes singing and opens her eyes and I want to keep looking at her and want to ask her to sing the song all over again. But obviously I don't do that, because not only would it appear outrageously desperate but also rude as I continue to stare at her. So I immediately take my eyes off her and say,

"Wow! You sing... really well. I mean... *wow!*"

"Thank you." She smiles shyly as she looks at me.

This is when we notice the loud sounds in the background. There is a total commotion among the students as Janvi is running around.

It has started to rain and the initial droplets are so big, they make quite a thumping sound as they hit the ground.

"Everyone under the tree," Mansi commands as she stands up. These teachers are so natural at this, aren't they – the ability to command people like this runs in their blood.

We have all clustered under the tree. It's raining real hard and the tree can no longer provide us shelter. Even bigger drops of water are now falling on our heads. Everything is good, I mean, I love being outside in the rain, it's one thing that has always made me happy since as far back as my memory can take me, but there is one real big problem here – all the books and teaching aids are getting damaged.

The missing man

It's quite a loss actually – everything that we had collected for the class is ruined. I don't think that the books are in readable condition anymore. And neither do the charts look that nice anymore. But it's ok, at the most we will have to put in some more money and buy some more stuff. It's not the end of the world. But now we have to make sure of one thing – we need a roof under which we can teach the kids – we need *a classroom*.

I am walking back to my house holding the carton which has the remains of all our class property.

I am looking straight ahead and I can see my house. And for some unknown reason, there are three to four people standing in front of the gate. They are talking among themselves and they are all wearing the same kind of clothes. Why would someone do that? I mean it's completely juvenile – I used to do this when I was what, 12 years old maybe. My friends and I would wear the same kind of clothes and then go roaming around in the market and other happening places. But I fail to understand why these people would do that – they are no kids, they are proper grown up men, and this is no happening place. And moreover, the colour they are wearing is not making them look good – it's khaki for heaven's sake. They should take fashion tips from Mansi; she always looks great and has a super dressing sense. Now I don't want them to start dressing up like *her*, but I am sure she can direct them to buy some cool stuff. But who are these people? Are they postmen? But why would someone send us so many letters that it would need too many postmen to deliver?! Maybe my fans! Maybe after the article came out, people wanted to send me letters and that happened in such huge volumes that so many postmen were needed to deliver them! Oh my God! This is so exciting!

I have reached the gate of my house. Ok, this is their lucky day – they are gonna get to meet *the* celebrity *in person*.

"May I help you?" I say as I put the carton down on the ground and look at them more carefully. They are no postmen, they are police officers! Maybe they have come to present me some bravery award. This is super cool!

"We are looking for Mr Rishabh Suri." One of them steps forward.

"Yes, that's me." A huge smile appears on my face. It's almost a reflex.

"I am Inspector Gurdeep."

"Nice to meet you Mr. Gurdeep." I extend my right hand forward.

"Yes," he replies as we shake hands and continues, "Mr. Rishabh, we are here for the ongoing investigation of a case. Mr. Sahota is missing. And from our sources we have found out that you were in touch with him."

OH MY GOD! WHAT?

"Missing... what do you mean?" How can he go missing? He is the kind of person who can make *other* people go missing. How can *he* go missing?"

"Missing meaning we are not able to locate his whereabouts. And we would really appreciate your co-operation in our investigation."

"Yes, sure."

* * *

I am in the office and I can't put my head to work.

I don't really know how I should feel about it. I mean for sure he was not a nice person. But that does not mean that I would want bad things to happen to him. I mean... that's all in the hands of God and... anyway, why am I thinking about it so much? I have told the police all I know and that is all I can do. They also took my fingerprint sample and said that it was only for the record. I was totally co-operative with them. Anyway, I must not think about it more. I should just wind up my work quickly at the office and go to my teacher's house – I am invited for tea at her place. (Hurray!) I really hope she offers me that famous chocolate cake of hers.

The teacher

Her house is as magnificent as I remember and I still fancy it as much as I used to, all those years ago. It's a very old house and very well maintained. And unlike Mr. Sahota, my teacher does not plan to make it look like a mall. She has taken care to ensure that all the features are wonderfully maintained. See, this is what people with values do – they conserve, they don't let culture die. We (my teacher and I) are in the front yard of the house and have been talking for over an hour now – it's amazing how one can reconnect with someone after so many years instantly. She used to be my favourite teacher back in school and I used to trouble her with my problems all the time. And she would listen to everything most patiently. And things are pretty much the same even today – she has been listening to me talk about everything I have done all these years since the second I entered her house. I am sitting on this wonderful garden *jhula* and Ma'am is sitting on a chair in front of me. I see the huge house in the background. There is a screen of arches that runs along the façade of the house with beautifully intricate capitols on the columns (which I absolutely love, by the way) and I can sense more than 10 rooms inside.

"That's a beautiful house you have." I can't hold back my admiration for the house.

Ma'am smiles as she puts the tea cup she was holding on the garden table in front of her.

"It's quite an old house. This year it will be completing 128 years," she says.

"Wow!"

"Quite some stories these walls can tell." She smiles as she looks at the house. "But it's very hard to maintain this house. I have done it for so many years, and I am tired now."

Silence.

"So, tell me, how's everything going? I can't congratulate you enough for your efforts," she says brightly.

"Thank you so much Ma'am. Things are good. What I am doing is really satisfying, it's so great teaching the kids. There are a few glitches that we need to take care of, but we should easily be able to handle it."

"Is it, like what?" she frowns lightly.

"Nothing big actually, it's just that… we conduct the classes in a park near my house and… today morning all our things were damaged in the rain. We are now trying to figure out… how to find a place… a shelter essentially, to teach the kids in."

"*Beta*, that is not a problem at all. You should have told me this earlier. I will ask the principal of our school and arrange a room for you. That is the least we can do to support your efforts."

"Thank you so much Ma'am." Smash! Talk about luck!

Got a room!

So, after the meeting with my teacher, I immediately call up Mansi and ask her to come a little early the next day for the class saying I have great news to share. (And obviously, I ask her to inform Janvi too.) I reach half an hour before time and Mansi comes 10 minutes later.

"Where is Janvi?" I ask.

"She wanted to sleep," Mansi smiled, "She said she doesn't mind knowing the 'great news' a little late."

"Ok." I look at her. God! Is she pretty? How does she always manage to look... so fresh?

"So?" she asks.

"Oh yes! The news! It's like the greatest thing ever – we got a room!"

She just looks at me and does not say anything.

Okay, that didn't sound right. Damn!

"I mean we have a classroom now for the kids. And that is what we will get the room for and... strictly for no other purpose," I stammer.

"Hey! That is great news!"

"I know!"

"Where are we getting the classroom? And how?"

"Long story, but the short of it is that my favourite teacher from school talked to the principal of the school who agreed to give us a classroom for one hour every morning for which I would have to take full responsibility."

"This is... tremendous!" she sounds really happy.

"I know!"

Ok, now that I have told her the great news, what are we supposed to do? Maybe I didn't need to call her to come early to share the news, now that I think of it – it took less than a minute to share.

We are sitting under a tree, the morning sun rays are slowly spreading out and everything feels super fresh. I realize this is one of the rare moments when Mansi and I are alone. I want to keep gazing at her but I must not do that – it's not polite.

"So, how's everything?" she asks.

"Things are good, all good, work is going fine, I am to… redesign for the client, who I got to know only yesterday has gone missing. Everything at home is just fine and you already know all the details about the classes we are conducting, so… that is pretty much it."

What is wrong with me? Why am I totally blabbering like this? This is not an interview.

She smiles.

"So, when are you getting married?" Oh my God! I have no sense; I have no sense at all as to how to make any moves!!! Why would I ever ask her that?

"I don't think that is gonna happen." She smiles again.

"Why? I… mean that it's a nice thing, isn't it – getting married?"

"For some people, yes. Anyway, you tell me, what about you? No girlfriend?"

"Me? No, no way!"

"Oh come on, I don't believe you. I know Natasha and you are *just friends*, but that does not say that there is no one else." She has a naughty smile on her face now.

"Well, it's not that I never had one, but we just broke up some time back."

"I am sorry, but what happened?… If you don't mind my asking."

I look at her and smile, "It's ok, she went abroad to do a Masters and... said that... she didn't like me that way anymore."

"I am sorry to hear that. Long distance relationships are tricky that way."

"It's ok," I shake it off with a smile, "You tell me, never been in a relationship?"

"Well, there was one guy," she takes a pause and continues, "Long time back. We were... so attached to each other. Then he got a job in Delhi and he wanted me to get a job there too, so that we could be together. I floated the idea at home and my parents were furious but I went anyway. When we reached there... he just... changed – he became a completely different person. After a few months I came back losing... all my trust in relationships. Relationships are... not for me. It's something that... I don't believe in anymore." Her voice is firm and she does not even look disturbed or upset as she speaks.

"I am sorry," I say.

"It's ok, we all have a past." She smiles.

* * *

Dear Rishabh,

I have been thinking about... us, a lot lately. Things shouldn't have ended the way they did. I came here and I got carried away with this new... culture. I was a total moron to say the things I said – to behave the way I did. It's just that... you have been everything for me, always. I don't know what I was thinking when I said that I don't want to be with you. In fact, I was not thinking then. But after you left, I realized that you were such an important part of my life – *you were my life*. And you still are. There is no one in this whole world who can ever take your place. No one can ever be as good as you. Please forgive me and come back. I don't know how to live without you… I don't know how to do anything without you.

Yours,

Superna.

? Why would she write to me now? I mean *now*, when things have actually begun to fall in place. This does not make any sense at all. I am in no mood to reply to her right now.

To kill a child

It's weird how everything starts to appear dull and sad when one thing goes wrong in your life. When would my relationship with Superna stop haunting me? Right when I had decided that my relationship with her was a thing of the past, she comes back. It's tough not to go back and start thinking how I had imagined my future with her, you know.

It's an extremely dull day today and even the office looks totally sloppy. It seems that something is wrong with everyone. Look at Savaray, even he looks upset today.

I toss my bag on the side table and ask him, "What's wrong with you?"

He is sitting next to the window. He turns to look at me, sighs heavily and goes back to looking out of the window saying, "Manju is pregnant."

"… I know but… that is a good thing, right? I mean now there will be four of you."

"She does not want the baby, she wants an abortion."

* * *

I haven't felt this zonked out in years. I am just not able to focus on work. How can someone do this? How can someone simply decide to kill a child? It's *not* a fair decision. No one has the right to do so. I won't let them do this – I will talk them out of it.

Savaray is sitting next to the window where he has been sitting all morning.

"Savaray, I think you should keep the child," I say, looking at him.

"I want to, but Manju says she does not."

"Why?"

"Because she says Krishna is still very young and she is still very weak."

Just then we hear the bell ring – the boss is here. With one quick involuntary movement, Savaray gets up and goes out. In less than a minute he comes back and says, "Sir is calling you."

In another minute, I am in Sir's office.

I am sitting in front of my boss, across the table on which the drawing that I have been working on is spread out.

He is looking at the drawing and shaking his head in a clearly pretentious manner.

"Rishabh, tell me something, did you choose architecture of your own will or were you forced into it?"

I am totally dumbstruck. I gape at him clueless.

He keeps looking at me, demanding an answer.

"It was my own decision, Sir..."

He continues shaking his head and says, "I don't understand then... where is your dedication for work, so many mistakes in the drawings?"

Now what am I supposed to say? I am too overwhelmed to know that the caretaker of your office is getting his child aborted and I cannot take my mind off it?

"One day you call in sick and go roaming around the town and then make drawings that are of no use to me!" he says, looking me right in the eye.

Oh my God! Now I know why he is behaving this way! He must have seen me somewhere that day when I was out with Natasha. This creature of the night roams around in the day too! Oh no!

He clears his throat and continues, "Rishabh, whatever you do in life, you must have strong reasons for that. I feel you still haven't found what you enjoy doing."

Is he kidding me? There can be no one, on the face of this earth, who would enjoy hand drafting on these gateway sheets which, by the way, are always conspiring to give paper cuts on your fingers.

"Anyway," he says, "you make these corrections that I have marked on the sheet and show it to me again."

* * *

I need to talk to someone about it. There is a child in the making and someone is gonna make it… stop living! I am in my room at home, sitting next to the window, gazing out at the garden.

I hear a knock on the door and turn to see who it is.

"Soup? You want soup?" It's Mom.

Why on earth would she suddenly want me to have soup?

"No," I reply dully.

She comes, sits next to me and asks, "How's work going?"

"It's going fine."

Now her eyes are peeping into me.

"If you want to talk about something, I am all ears."

I take a deep breath as I think about whether I should discuss it with her or not.

"The caretaker at my office; his wife is expecting a baby. And she wants to abort it." I sigh.

She keeps looking at me and does not say anything as if she knows that I am not done talking.

"Is there no way we can save that child? She does not want to keep the child. That's ok, what if she delivers the kid and *we* adopt the kid? The child, he… deserves a life, he deserves to… come into this world. They can't... murder the child like that!"

"Rishabh, look at me," she says as I raise my eyes from the ground to look at her.

"I understand what you feel. And I know how terrible it is. But it's her life. And she must have her reasons for what she has decided. It's very difficult to raise children; there are so many reasons, monetary issues, health issues. And it's also understandable if they want to have only one child and raise him giving the best they can. We cannot make her do something that she does not want to."

I look at my Mom and there is only one thing that runs in my mind – if only I were a vampire and I could compel Manju to deliver the child and then kidnap the new born kid as soon as he was born and run away somewhere.

* * *

Dear Superna,

I always asked for a second chance, I always felt that life would not be life without you. Perhaps that was because at that time I didn't really understand what life actually meant. I cannot say that I understand life completely now, that would be foolish. But yes, the picture is slightly clearer now.

Life isn't all about finding a girlfriend and wanting to spend the rest of '*life*' together: there is a lot more to it than that. I had a lot of time in the past few weeks to reflect on things. And one of the things that I realized was that love is not something that ends the way our relationship ended. It is something so strong and deep that not even death can kill it. What we had was not love; it was a frantic desperation to find a companion. I have realized this, and I hope you will realize it too one day.

Wish you all the best for everything you wish for.

Yours sincerely,

Rishabh Suri

It's a crying shame how we think our tiny problems are the end of our world when people around us are actually battling for their lives. It's time for me to shake these things off.

The changing children

It's amazing how much these kids have changed. I remember how terribly out of control the lot was on the first day and just look at them today – they are all sitting nicely at their desks in the classroom, like tiny tamed lions at a circus. It's only two of us today – Mansi and me [Janvi said that she has fallen (sick)]. I think it's a plain lie; she is just not interested in this thing anymore. And it seriously does not make any difference as we are facing no problem at all conducting the class. Even I took charge for some time and gave a few lessons to the children.

We have a proper 45 minute class and then take the children out of the school in the most disciplined manner. Actually the environment and the set-up makes a lot of difference – the kids are way more civilized and I firmly believe that it's because they are sitting in a school.

All the children have left and we are standing at the gate. Obviously we are supposed to leave and go (to our respective homes), but we stand there, each waiting for the other to say 'bye.'

"It's funny how things change with time, isn't it?" I say, somewhat amused.

She gives me a searching look, as if asking me to explain what I meant.

"I mean it was not that long ago when I came to this town and was making desperate attempts to fit in and make friends. And just see how well things have turned out now," I say.

"True." She smiles and looks at the ground.

Ok, I have miserably failed to strike up a conversation.

"We should... go." I stammer.

"Yeah."

* * *

It's all so logical – everything follows a graph, even life. Just take the example of *my* life for instance – yesterday I was so upset about the killing of the unborn kid and today I am already in the process of getting over it – I have touched the trough and now am soaring up to happiness. I am on my way home and I am sure today is gonna be a wonderful day.

Suspect (for murder)?

Life follows a pattern that is totally absurd and illogical and makes no sense whatsoever! I reached home and again found the police waiting for me. They are taking me to the police station and are saying that they want to ask me a few questions regarding Mr. Sahota's disappearance.

I am sitting in the police jeep and the most terrible thoughts are storming through my mind. I quickly need to find a way to escape from these police people. Clearly they have been working on the case and have got no leads of any kind. Now they want to just shut the case by falsely accusing someone and they have picked me! *God!* They are gonna take me to some lonely... fields outside the town and just shoot me and say that they had to kill me in an encounter as I was trying to escape and was attempting to kill them too! God please save me! What am I gonna do? *What am I gonna do?*

The jeep comes to a halt and one of the fat scary officials comes and opens the door for me. It's just like how they treat an object of sacrifice before a ritual – serve the sacrifice most royally and then, BAM!

* * *

They take me inside the police station which is like the weirdest building I have ever seen – it is beyond me to register the rooms that seem scattered all around the central 'lobby'. Like a sheep I simply follow the man in khakhi in front of me who leads me to a not-so-tidy room and asks me to sit.

There are some three people in the room and I sit among them even as some whispering goes on around me. After a while as I realise I'm bathing in my sweat, Inspector Gurdeep comes and sits in front of me and bends down to take something out of a drawer.

"Mr. Suri, do you recognize this?" he asks as he puts a gun in a transparent polythene bag in front of me.

Oh my God! I am in deep trouble! I am in the deepest trouble ever! I must think of something! Must cook up a story *right now*! But my mind does not run so fast. Damn! I am so dumb!

"Yes," I mutter.

He looks at me as his eyes shoot a 1000 questions.

"But listen, I can explain," I say, looking at him with eyes as wide as saucers.

He does not say anything and continues to stare at me.

"I know this gun, I mean, I recognize it. I had gone to Mr. Sahota's house to take some measurements as he wanted to renovate his house."

The stupid face of Kavita flashes in front of me as I say the word 'measurements'; the way she pushed me against the wall and behaved so obscenely. But there is no way I am gonna tell them anything about it – that secret will go with me to my grave.

"And there was this... wonderful piece of antique furniture that I happened to lay my eyes on and I was so... strongly attracted to it that I had to go take a closer look."

As I continue, I see a skewed expression on Mr. Gurdeep's face and I don't even want to know where his mind is taking him.

"And I just happened to open one of the drawers of the table where I saw this gun," I say as I take a deep breath.

"So you just saw the gun?" he questions.

Silence.

"That does not explain how your fingerprints got onto the gun."

Damn! They matched my fingerprints! They said they were taking my fingerprint samples only for their record. They are such creeps! I look at everyone around me and I feel that this is the most horrific experience I have ever had. The man sitting in front of me is scaring the life out of me and the three other police officers towering around me are gonna kill me with plain anxiety.

"That is because I... did take the gun in my hands." The inspector continues to look at me, waiting for me to explain.

This is really gonna sound stupid.

"I had... never seen a real gun before," I say, grinning sheepishly. "So when I saw this, I... took it in my hands. I have always been a great 007 fan. And I just wanted to see how I looked with a gun in my hand when I posed like James Bond. So I... held the gun for a while and posed in the mirror for some time. But it was only for a few seconds, I swear. Mrs. Sahota came in then and I immediately put the gun back. I didn't do anything else." God! I want to die now – I am so embarrassed!

"Mr. Suri, do you realize the seriousness of the matter?" he asks, sounding like a total cop from one of those detective shows on TV.

I gape back at him and don't say a word.

"Mr. Sahota is missing. And we don't know if he is alive or dead.

I hope you understand this."

I gulp in sheer fretfulness. I understand he holds me as a suspect. But I do not know anything – *I am innocent!*

"You can leave now Mr. Suri. We will let you know if we need your help again."

!!! What have I gotten myself into this time!!!

Freaked out!

Rishabh: i am so dead. i have no idea how i am gonna get out of it this time. I AM DEAD!!!

Natasha: would you just calm down and tell me what the hell happened?

Rishabh: i am the accused! i am being accused of murder!

Natasha: rishabh, chill.

Rishabh: ok ☹

Natasha: now tell me what happened.

Rishabh: you remember the gun incident at the sahota house?

Natasha: yes.

Rishabh: the police discovered that. and they said i am a suspect! they are accusing me of murder! someone is trying to frame me! why would someone want to frame me? i have never done anything bad to anyone! why would someone want to do that?!

Natasha: rishabh, did they say that?

Rishabh: say what?

Natasha: that you are being accused of murder?

Rishabh: umm… no.

Natasha: then why are you freaking out?

Rishabh: coz they said that they don't know if he is alive or dead and i was a suspect!

Natasha: did he say that?

Rishabh: no. he just said that he needs my help for the investigation.

Natasha: so u are neither a suspect nor the accused. and for heaven's sake, learn the meaning of the words 'accused' and 'suspect'. and you will have to google it, i am not gonna explain it to you.

Rishabh: ok ☹

Natasha: yes.

Rishabh: there is only one thing in my life that is good right now – the classes for the children. i don't know what i would do if that fell off the track too.

Natasha: you need to do only one thing – STOP FREAKING OUT!

* * *

The worst has happened. Hell has broken loose!!! Strange diseases are spreading around the country; some scary tick fever.

They say it's come from Africa, is spread by ticks and is quite fatal. The principal of the school where we conduct the classes has asked me to meet her. I am waiting outside her office and am absolutely clueless as to what she is gonna say. Maybe she wants to give me some useful tips on how to stay away from the disease.

An average looking lady (with quarter plates for specs) comes and informs me that Principal ma'am wants to see me now.

It's a huge room – definitely more spacious than what one person would require.

She looks at me and says, "Please come Mr. Rishabh. Have a seat."

I sit and want her to get to business right away.

"How are you?" she asks.

"I am good, how are you?"

"I am good."

Silence.

"Mr. Rishabh there has been a problem. There have been reports of certain diseases lately. I really appreciate your effort at teaching underprivileged children. But the parents of the students of this school have raised their worries about hygiene issues and... the school board has suggested that you discontinue the classes."

Misunderstood

It's a cruel and unjust world we live in. I still can't believe that the school has asked us to stop using their classrooms to deliver our classes. My life is completely over. There is no hope for anything anymore. And to top everything, there was an article in the papers today about the case of Mr. Sahota. Now Mrs. Sahota is being accused of being unfaithful to her husband and is being questioned for her husband's disappearance. And if you ask me, it's quite possible actually. She only needs to catch sight of a man to start hitting on him. Maybe it's actually *she* who has kidnapped him. But why would she kidnap him? I mean, kidnapping one's own husband? That does not make sense. She must have murdered him; and that too with the same gun. Oh my God! *She is the one who is trying to frame me*!

I am at Mansi's place and we are here to discuss the fate of the classes – what we are gonna do about it. She is in the kitchen cooking something as I am hungry. I am in the living room and there are old photo albums and pictures scattered all around. Supposedly Mansi was feeling very nostalgic and was going through all of her old pictures.

I can't help picking up a few and looking at them. She really looked cute when she was a kid. I find a picture in which she is grinning at the camera, her hair in two cute little pigtails. In another picture she has the same grin but the only difference is that one of her front teeth is missing and the pigtails are longer. I can't help smiling – she looks adorable.

There are so many pictures – family photographs, pictures with friends, pictures of birthday parties, and pictures of holidays somewhere in the mountains. All the faces are new to me and I don't recognize anyone. I flip through one full album and suddenly one face catches my eye. It's an old photo in which Mansi is quite young. There is this man who is standing next to her father, or at least I assume the other man is her father, owing to all the other pictures I saw. The man has broad, handsome features. I immediately recognize his face – how can I ever miss it – he is the man who has gone missing. *He is Mr. Sahota*!

"I couldn't pull off anything better than this so quickly," Mansi says as she puts a tray in front of me on a table. I am so shocked that I don't even notice what she has brought for us to eat.

I sit quietly for a few seconds but cannot hold myself back for long. I ask her, "Mansi, do you know Mr. Sahota?"

Silence.

"Do you know him?" I repeat.

She flops on a chair in front of me and avoids looking at me directly.

* * *

Mr. Sahota is Mansi's uncle, can you beat that? At least I can't. I am still at her place and she has explained things (or so she says). According to her, it would not have made any difference if she had told me that he is her uncle. It would have only resulted in a more stressful situation. She is actually quite troubled because her uncle has gone missing and no one has any leads. The punch of anger and betrayal that I felt when I first saw the pictures of Mansi with Mr. Sahota has now faded and I now feel only sympathy for her. She is troubled. She also said that she had never wanted to hide this fact from me, why else would she leave all the pictures lying around like that openly. Also she said that she was planning to tell me about him later today.

I am looking at her and I can actually believe all she is saying.

"I was his favourite niece. I still am..." she says, as she smiling at me with eyes that shine with the tears that she is trying to hold back.

There is a moment of silence as we both sit there and sip the tea she had prepared minutes ago.

"He used to bring so many kinds of chocolates and I used to save them for later and then eat them one by one slowly. I would never share them with anyone," she says, laughing a little.

"I am sorry for... yelling at you earlier," I apologize. I swear I must stop watching the telly. All those shows in which people keep screaming at each other all the time as they flash each shot three times without fail, really push you to force drama into your real life. "And I am really sorry about your uncle," I continue.

"It's ok. I know he is fine. He is a very strong person. No one can take him down so easily," she says. She has never sounded so serious before.

"I am so sure of that," I say.

"And you formed a very wrong idea about him when you first met him," she continues. "He is very sensitive to child labour issues himself. He had that child at his place because his parents had forced him to go to the city and work."

She takes a sip from the tea cup in her hands and continues, "And he always teaches the kid who works at his place himself. Their previous servant gave the 12th board exams a few months back and now has a job at a cyber café. It's just that he is a little harsh with them at times but that is his way of teaching them how tough the world is gonna be with them."

I am a terrible person. *I am the worst person I know*! Mr. Sahota is such a great person – he would get chocolates for his little niece and he teaches underprivileged kids. And I mistook him for everything! But wait a minute. His wife, she is a total... vamp! I must unmask her for Mansi right now!

"But Mansi, Mrs. Sahota, she is not a nice person..." I trail off into silence as I see Mansi looking at me. I narrate the whole incident to her.

"Kavita Mami and Mamu have the best relationship. There is no way what you are thinking can be true," she says, "She must have played a prank on you."

I stare at her speechless.

"She must have seen how nervous you were that day and she must have just... played along. I read the article in the newspaper today. The police, with the media, are just cooking up a story as they are not able to solve the case. She is just a fun loving person, maybe naughty at times. But she can never be unfaithful like that."

I hear her out but what she says does not convince me.

The affair

This whole thing is becoming more serious and complicated day by day. I got a call from the police people at around 5 o' clock in the evening and had to come to the police station straight after office hours. I don't even know what they are gonna ask (or do with me) today. I have heard so many terrible stories about things getting nasty during interrogation. And those are not false or made up stories – they all come from genuine sources. One of my friend's friends was caught with a pistol without a license. He was kept in the lock-up for over a week and was beaten up quite badly.

Just then I see the Chief I now recognize march into the building and go straight to a dark and dingy room. The place looks even creepier in the night. I don't understand why they won't clean it up. There are cobwebs hanging in all the corners of the room. I know they trap flies and mosquitoes but they also catch dust. What if they decide to keep me here for a week? I would surely fall sick. And I know for a fact that they would not call for a doctor or take me to the hospital. I would just... die then. God! I am so dead. *I am so dead*!!!

One of the fat scary khaki guys comes out and says, "Mr. Rishabh, please come in."

* * *

The room looks scarier each time I enter it. There is a strange eerie feel to it today. I am sitting in front of Mr. Gurdeep as he is filling something in, in a huge register of his, completely ignoring my presence. After five minutes or so, he loudly slams the register shut and looks at me.

"So, Mr. Rishabh, we meet again," he says.

"I guess so." I feel awkward.

"Mr. Rishabh, how well do you know Mrs. Kavita Sahota?"

Can I hide somewhere? Can I just run somewhere???!!!

"Not that well... not really... no."

"Mr. Rishabh, I would really appreciate it if you were honest with us. It would make things easier for both of us."

"She is my client... or was – I am not sure if they want to hire us for the project anymore, or if the project is even on anymore. And yes, she is my friend's aunt. But I don't think that adds or subtracts anything. I have just met her once, that's it."

I have told him everything right? I can't think of anything else to tell him – that's all I know about Mrs. Sahota.

"You are claiming that you don't have any kind of intimate relation with her."

"Yes sir."

There is no way he knows about the prank she played on me that day. Only if she is a big blabber mouth and went around telling everyone about it herself, only then would he know.

"Then how do you explain this?" he snaps as he throws a set of pictures on the table with the kind of style and sophistication they show in the movies.

I sit there flabbergasted as I gape at the pictures. The pictures are of the exact moment when Mrs. Sahota has pinned me against the wall and is about to touch me here and there. I am beyond stunned as I wonder where the hell these pictures have come from. Can I just say these are fabricated?

People do wonders with Photoshop these days.

"Mr. Sahota had a CCTV in his bedroom," Mr. Gurdeep says.

What? Who does that? Who keeps a CCTV camera in his bedroom? I am sorry but I find it real hard to believe that Mr. Sahota is a nice person anymore. I mean... *who does that?*

"Sir... I can explain this." I stammer as he looks at me with his arms folded across his chest.

"It's a just a prank that Mrs. Sahota played on me that day. I swear. And other people know about this... joke too. If you want, I can ask them to explain it to you. Seriously, I swear, there is nothing going on between Mrs. Sahota and me. And even if there had been anything, I would have told you. Why would I lie or hide about something like that? If we had been in love, I would have been honest and open about it. Why would I ever want to hide it?" I look directly into his eyes and say this. I am being totally honest – cross-my-heart-and-hope-to-die kind of honest, and he *has* to believe me. And God! How can he even think like that? She is almost my mother's age.

"Mr. Rishabh the only reason we are being so gentle with you is your recent action with the child labour issues and your attempts to teach the underprivileged children," he says with his bloodshot eyes fixed on me. "But if we find any solid proof against you, things would be very different."

* * *

Rishabh: that was no way to talk to me. he had no right to talk to me like that!

Natasha: you don't need to feel threatened. they can't do

anything. and if they ever threaten or even touch you, just let me know. i know how to set these people right. just because they are not able to solve the case, does not mean that they can trouble innocent people.

Rishabh: you mean they need to harm me first, only then you would do something? can't you just do something now and set the whole thing right?

Natasha: no rishabh i can't do that. God! would you ever grow up?

Rishabh: huh!

Natasha: anyway, let me just look into the whole thing myself once, i'll see what we should do then.

Rishabh: ok.

Natasha: ya.

Rishabh: and thank god mom does not know anything about this. she would have created a mayhem over the whole thing.

Out of control

"What the hell is this?" It's morning and I have just stepped out of my room. Mom is standing in front of me with fire in her eyes and a newspaper in her hands.

"I leave you alone for a few days thinking that finally you have grown up and have become responsible handling a job and all, and what you do is go out there and become a criminal?!"

I take the newspaper that she is shoving in my face and look at it. Oh God! Hell has broken loose!!! What should I do? This cannot be happening! *This just cannot be happening to me!* They have splashed the whole story in the newspapers today. Apparently it is a big deal as Mr. Sahota was an NRI. It's almost a half-page article. They are really highlighting the case.

"Mom, I am not a criminal," I stammer as I struggle to defend myself.

"Then what is this? What the hell is this." She is screaming now.

I can't breathe. I am suffocating. Where has all the oxygen gone! God! And my stomach is twisting now! Spasm! *Spasm*!!!

"Mom, I can explain..."

"You can explain all you want but it's not going to change the fact that you are involved in this!" she shouts as she cuts me off.

"Mom, please calm down. I am not involved in anything. I am just helping them out with the investigation."

"That is *not* what the paper is saying," she snaps as she snatches the paper back from me.

"Mom, please, calm down." I take the paper back from her and try to figure out what she is saying.

Oh my God! They have published the bedroom pictures of Mrs. Sahota and me! This person is so dead! The journalist, whoever has done this, is *soo dead*. I am gonna get this dude (or dudette) fired!

"Everyone was right. They were all correct. I was the only fool." Mom cries, "I was the foolish one not to listen to them. They told me, again and again, that I should get you married. I *believed* that you meant it when you said that you want to establish your career first. But you went *ruining* your family name for this..." Mom holds her tongue as she is about to say something really nasty.

"Mom, chill. It's not what..."

She cuts me off and shoots, "Do you know she is just five years younger than me? Do you realize what the society calls people who behave like you?"

Ok, now she is just fulfilling her desire to make her life appear more dramatic. (Yes, it runs in my family.) I am in no case gonna respond to that.

"Mom, she was just playing a prank on me, she was just joking." I don't really believe what I say, but right now I can't explain it in any other way.

"This looks like a joke to you? Is that what you would call this? A joke?" she yells and shoves the newspaper in my face again.

I need to bring this situation under control now, by all means.

"Mom," I go to her, hold her by her shoulders and look into her eyes, "Please listen to me; I am not involved in it the way you are... imagining. It's just a huge... titanic misunderstanding."

She is looking at me and is silent – she looks a little eased now. After a while she says, "Do you realize they are accusing you of murder?"

Everything plays out all over again in my mind – from all the scolding from Natasha to all the pages I had googled finding the 'technical' and 'legal' information.

"Yes, but... not legally," I say with a skewed expression.

* * *

Natasha: ok, so i have been following up on the case and things do look slightly *tangled*.

Rishabh: i saw the movie, it was nice. you've seen it, right?

Natasha: rishabh, i need you to be serious for once.

Rishabh: … ok ☹

Natasha: now listen to me, all the evidence is going against you. we need more evidence to prove your case. and why the hell did you ever go and take that gun in your hands. that was like the most… outrageously stupid thing i have ever heard anyone do!

Rishabh: it's the media's fault, not mine. why did they project james bond like that?

Natasha: God! why did i even go there? anyway, you need to do 2 things, #1 try fixing up a meeting with mrs. sahota and try getting some leads from her.

Rishabh: ok

Natasha: and take mansi's help to fix the meeting.

Rishabh: ya, i should do that. you are so intelligent!

Natasha: yes rishabh, it's only a genius who can think of that.

Rishabh: :/

Natasha: and #2 try talking to your kid (whatever his name is. and don't you start about respect and names again) and find out how he reached your town.

Rishabh: yes, we are working on two cases now – the disappearance of mr. sahota and the terrible case of child trafficking.

Natasha: yes, and get back to me with the info, we'll see what to do next.

Rishabh: natasha

Natasha: what?

Rishabh: am i going to jail?

Natasha: shut up!

Rishabh: natasha

Natasha: now what?

Rishabh: thank you ☺

Natasha: ?

Rishabh: for everything. you have been such a great friend. i always keep troubling you all the time with all my problems and never listen to any of yours. but you are always there to help me with all your heart. thank you ☺

Natasha: ? what's gotten into you today? are you ok?

Rishabh: yes, i am totally fine. and i know i owe you bigtime. you are the only one who can pull me together and put some sense into my head. thank you ☺

Natasha: you are welcome. (you are not drunk, right?)

Rishabh: GGRRRRRRRRRRR!

Natasha: joke, joke. you are a very dear friend of mine and i know for a fact that you have a pure heart. i saw that the day we met. one needs people like you in one's life to believe that the world is not all that bad a place to live in. and i want things to remain that way.

Rishabh: you are the best.

Natasha: thank you ☺ and you are not that bad either.

Must dig out the truth

I am going to jail! I am so going to jail! I got Natasha's subtle hint last night. There is no way I can prove my innocence in this case now. I am so stuck and so… numb that I don't even know how I am feeling. I tried talking to Ramesh today morning and he explained the whole thing in total detail to me. (Kids these days are smart!) How it works is that there is a guy from their village who works here in this city. He has connections and keeps a check on who needs a servant/helper for their house. Once he gets a query, he gets a kid from his village and hands him/her over to the party. And from what I gather from Ramesh, it seems that the kids are also quite eager to come to the city, so it's not like he gets the children against their wishes. (It's not criminal from that point of view.) But that's not all; there is a major twist in the whole thing – the guy who gets the kids from the village works as a housekeeper at the Sahotas'. Now I haven't seen or met him during my disastrous 'measurement' visit to the house, but I am sure gonna ask about him today. So if Mr. Sahota is not all innocent, unlike what Mansi says, this housekeeper guy might only be Mr. Sahota's puppet. And this is what I have come to find out – I am at the Sahota residence. (Yes, arranging the meeting with Mrs. Sahota was a piece of cake – all thanks to Mansi.) I am keeping my fingers crossed, I am praying to God that Mrs. Sahota does not throw herself at me the way she did last time. Although

Mansi told me about the whole thing being a joke, who knows the real story, right? What if Mrs. Sahota actually has the hots for me? You never know what kind of men some women might like. Maybe that macho kind isn't her type? What if she likes younger, ordinary, more believable kinds? And I know for a fact that a lot of people find architects hot. I mean just take Franky's example (Frank Lloyd Wright I mean.) There was nothing hot about him. And I am not saying it just like that, if you don't believe me, go check his pictures on the net – he was *really* short! But they say that he was notorious for sleeping with each of his client's wives. And I am not thinking all this because I *want* Mrs. Sahota to sleep with me. No, that is so not the case, definitely not – I have high ethics. I mean if we were to sleep around with every other person we came across, what would be the difference between us and wild animals? So I am not at all hoping for Mrs. Sahota to hit on me. Not even if that would boost my self-confidence.

I am finding it hard to pilot my train of thoughts when Mrs. Sahota finally comes and sits on the sofa in front of me.

I stand up as a gesture of respect as soon as I see her.

"Good morning Mr. Suri." She greets me with a smile that essentially looks hollow – her husband's disappearance is for sure eating her up.

"Good morning ma'am, how are you?"

"I am good, thank you." She nods graciously.

I fumble through my thoughts to say something appropriate, "I am sorry about the situation."

She smiles back and says, "It's ok, hard times fall upon each one of us." She is a real strong woman, I can sense how terribly disturbed she is but I don't see her eyes welling up or anything – she is so much in control. I do not want to go beating around the bush so I straightaway ask her,

"I want to help solve the case of your husband's disappearance. And it would really help if you would tell me what exactly happened on the day he disappeared."

She takes a deep breath and says, "Mr. Sahota looked a little troubled for a few days before he went missing. There was something on his mind that he wasn't willing to share, I tried so many times to find out, but he didn't say a thing." She takes a pause, looks at me and continues, "It actually started the day you came to our house."

I look at her blankly, completely unaware of the expression I should hold. I am a terrible person – I am the reason all this is happening. Why the hell could I simply not shut my trap and not over react the way I did. Mr. Sahota would have taken care of Ramesh. Mansi said he would have.

"I am really sorry Ma'am…"

"It's ok, it's not your fault." She cuts me off and continues, "one day he just got up and said that he was going hunting with his friends and would be off for a few days. I didn't ask him anything as I thought it was a good idea and that it would take his mind off the things that were troubling him. He just went out in his jeep and… has not returned yet." She looks at me and now her eyes are shiny.

"But Ma'am, he has gone missing and we need to find him. We must do something!"

How can we not find him? We can find… anything if we search properly. They say we can even find *God* if we search correctly.

After a short pause, I ask, "There must be some way to find him?"

She looks at me silently and I can almost hear the thoughts that must be running in her mind – why am I so bothered? I almost feel like explaining. I almost feel like saying that I mistook him for a bad person. He is a really nice person and nice things should happen to him. He has been missing for over two weeks and no one has been able to get to him. This is not his usual behaviour. No one knows what condition he must be in. We *have* to do something to find him. But I don't say anything.

Finally she speaks up, "We have a... farm house, around 90 kilometers from here, at a place called Nandugahr. It's some 30 kilometers away from a small piece of forestland." She takes an awkward pause and continues, "Whenever Mr. Sahota goes hunting, he makes that farmhouse his base." After another pause, she avoids eye contact and I can sense her unwillingness in saying what she is saying, "He must have gone there this time too if he went hunting."

I look at her as my mind suddenly starts to race and make strategies to find Mr. Sahota.

After a short pause, she continues, "But the police have already searched the whole place and so have I, none of us found any clues. Going there would not be of any use."

I look at her and for some reason, I feel that she is hiding something.

"There was something more I wanted to ask," I say. "Your house keeper, what's his name?"

"Vijay"

"Yes, I have never seen him. Does he stay here?"

"He has gone for his brother's wedding. It's been over a month now. You know how these people are," she replies.

"Ma'am, you know that he is suspected to be involved in a major case of child trafficking?"

She says with a sigh, "I don't understand what the police are up to. Vijay has been like a member of our family. We would have known if any such thing was true."

"I am sorry Ma'am, but I didn't get this information from the police."

"I don't think what you are saying is true," she says.

I look into her eyes and I don't feel that she is lying.

* * *

Rishabh: she didn't hit on me, she didn't hit on me at all this time.

Natasha: ? don't you think the whole thing is going a little overboard now?

Rishabh: what? i was just hoping that all that she did, it wasn't just a joke and she did actually find me... attractive.

Natasha: do you know how sick you sound right now?

Rishabh: huh, what would you understand? you are not the one who has never, ever got a single compliment in his entire life. how would you understand, natasha?

Natasha: rishabh, you are looking very hot today. happy? now you can't say you have never got any compliment.

Rishabh: yes i can, coz this one doesn't count as you can't see me.

Natasha: God! get over it already! we have more important things to discuss.

Rishabh: FINE!

Natasha: thank you. now would you enlighten me about the whole matter? what did kavita tell you?

Rishabh: see, i'll tell you, i have got it all figured out. mr. sahota went hunting. and that is where he went missing. we can't call him up and ask where he is coz his cell phone is not working. i have a strong feeling that he got separated from his friends as they were hunting. i am hoping that there has not been a *7 khoon maaf* scenario and none of his friends fed him to a hungry panther. rather, i am hoping more for a *127 hour* scenario, i am hoping that he is just lost in the jungle and has seen enough *man v/s wild* on discovery to know how to survive in the jungle till we go and find him before he would need to cut off his arm to save his life. we just need to find out what areas he generally goes hunting in. now as he didn't tell anyone whom he was going with (people don't learn from anything from the movies, do they?) we would have to figure out and go find him. i have already started making a list of all the things i would need to take along with me when i go on this search operation.

Natasha: God! someone please give me a break!

Rishabh: what? it's a simple case. and i have almost solved it.

Natasha: rishabh, i need you to find out more details about that agent/housekeeper guy and hand over all that information to the police first of all. What he is doing is illegal and he needs to be stopped. meanwhile i am gonna try to figure out what to do next.

Rishabh: ok, and by the way, there is this mysterious farmhouse too, that mr. sahota apparently uses as his base whenever he goes hunting. i have a strong feeling there are ghosts living in that house and they have transported mr. sahota to some other realm. I think we would have to call sam and dean to bring him back.

Natasha: sam and dean?

Rishabh: the wenchester brothers? they're from that unbelievably great tv show – *supernatural.* do you even know anything?

Natasha: God! You have started watching that show again?

Rishabh: ? they just started a new season! how could I ever stay away from it? you know what? maybe i can myself become a demon hunter (or whatever they call themselves) and get rid of all the evil spirits!!! that would be super cool! i would drive around from one town to another in a vintage car just like them! It would be the ultimate fantasy come true!

Natasha: there you go again!

Rishabh: ha ha! no, but on a serious note, i am planning to visit the farmhouse to look for clues.

Natasha: clues as to whether there are any evil spirits there?

Rishabh: :P

Natasha: don't go there alone, or the ghosts might just transport you to that other realm too. then both you and mr. sahota would be stuck there for eternity.

Rishabh: ya, I was thinking of taking mansi along. she would know the way to the place *and* she would know the place inside out too. i have already asked her to ask for the keys to the farmhouse from mrs. sahota.

Natasha: hmm, nice. but don't go hitting on her when you are alone with her there :P

Rishabh: oh! puhlease!

Natasha: oh! puhleeease!

It's not stealing!

Mansi and I are at a coffee shop. She had a word with Mrs. Sahota and wants to tell me something about it.

The Assam tea I had ordered has been served in a nice white cup on a saucer along with the Choco-Mocha Mansi had ordered. I offer the tall glass of coffee to Mansi and ask,

"So, did you ask Kavita Aunty for the keys?"

"... Yes," she hesitates as she sips her coffee. I look at her silently, waiting for her to continue.

"She said," she finally speaks up, "that there was no use going to the farmhouse as she had already been there." She avoids eye contact.

"Did you insist?" I ask.

"Yes I did. She refused to give the keys," she says as she sighs.

"*No* this cannot *be*, we have to get the keys!" I exclaim with utter desperation. Mansi is looking back at me with her big round eyes. She says nothing but I can sense what's going on in her mind – there is nothing more she can do.

"Mansi, please try to understand, there is something in that farmhouse that is keeping us away from finding your uncle. I have a very strong hunch about it and I swear it's strong. I don't know why Aunty is hiding it from us, but there is a clue there, *I just know it.*"

I look at Mansi, concentrating with all my might, to convince her to bring the keys.

"What do you want me to do Rishabh?" she finally speaks up, "Just go to her house and *steal* the keys?"

"Yes," I utter as she looks back at me shocked.

"I mean, no," I stammer. "I mean, just get the impression of the keys on a soap. That way the keys won't go missing and we would have a set of them for ourselves. Haven't you seen any crime thrillers at all?"

The filthy liar

So it turns out that if I wish to go to the mystery farmhouse, I would have to spend the night there. (I told Mansi that I am planning to visit the farmhouse to hunt for clues and asked her if she could come along. She became all emotional and said that she would come along as that was the least she could contribute in the effort to find her uncle.) It's a four hour plus drive to the place and going there and coming back all in one day can work out only if I drive at night, which I never do. What? It's like the unsafest thing ever! There are thugs! And terrible truck drivers on the road who are high on drugs and drive with their eyes closed! And I am not even exaggerating. There is no way I am gonna drive in the night. And this essentially means that I would have to spend the night at the farmhouse. Now don't get me wrong, I am not planning this because I have… things in mind for Mansi. I am planning this because it's the best (and safest) for both of us. And that is the truth. Although I have a strong feeling that the whole cosmos is conspiring for us to be together, but right now, I don't have anything like that in my mind. (No, seriously, otherwise why would both of us be *forced* to spend a night at a lonely farmhouse? Or why would her uncle come to my office as a client, then go missing and out of all the people in the world only I would get involved in this very case?)

Anyway, I have worked everything out and all is set. Now I have to cook up a story to tell Mom so that she does not get suspicious about the whole thing and just lets me go. She is never gonna let me go if she finds out where I am going and why. So I am simply gonna tell her that there is an official trip, that I have to go measure up a place for a project.

I walk into the living room where Mom is sitting on a sofa, reading the newspaper wearing her specs and is beyond engrossed in it.

"Mom, I have to go to a site tomorrow," I say.

"Ok, what site?" she asks without looking up.

"It's for a project at the office. I would have to leave sometime in the afternoon. It's a four hour plus drive to the place so I would have to stay the night there."

She raises her head and looks at me over the frame of her glasses. After a few seconds, she says, "Ok." And goes back to reading the paper. She does not suspect a thing. She is so innocent – she thinks that I am telling her the truth. And she thinks that… I am also that innocent.

I am a terrible person. I am the most terrible person breathing on the face of this earth. *I am lying to my own mother!* Lying is the highest degree of disrespect one can subject anyone to. And I am doing that to my very own mother? My own *blood*? No! I cannot hold it back – I can't do this. If I just let this be and simply walk out of this room, the guilt of this action is gonna haunt me forever – *for the rest of my life!*

"Mom." I almost whisper.

She looks up at me again.

"I am not going to the site tomorrow."

"You mean you would be coming home at the regular time then?"

She looks slightly confused now.

"No. Actually I am going, but... I am not going to any site. I mean, I am going to a *site*, but it's not a *work* site as I just said."

She looks at me as she takes off her specs now. This means that she has all her focus on what I am saying now.

"I am... going to a farmhouse that the Sahotas own." I have started talking, and I am not sure if I should be doing this.

"I am going there to... investigate... the case..."

"ARE YOU CRAZY?" she cuts me off.

"Mom, try to understand, the police has been working on the case and they have not been able to find any leads. And to top it all, they are suspecting me..."

"Which is all the more reason that you should stay away from all this!" She is really getting hyper now. I can see she has already started breathing heavily.

"Mom, try to understand. They can't arrest me or anything – they have no solid proof against me."

"Yeah, right. And you are going there to prepare some for them like you always do?" She is flipping like nobody's business – she is trembling with anxiety now.

"Mom…"

"You need to stay away from this, do you understand?" she cuts me off again.

Ok, I need to calm her down first. And then explain. I go sit down next to her and say,

"Mom, listen. I am safe; nothing is going to happen to me. I am not 10 years old anymore, I can take care of myself. And even if I fail, I know you are there to watch my back. I don't think the police are doing their bit properly. I just want to go to the place, and see if I find any clue that can help us solve the case." Please let me go!!!

It's working – she has calmed down. She is breathing fine now and she is not shivering anymore.

There is silence for a while and then she speaks up, "But Rishabh, going there alone and spending the night there, it does not sound like the sanest thing to do."

"I am not going there alone; Mansi would be going with me."

Suddenly her eyes are like saucers again and she bursts out,

"I am going with you!"

Mom & Mansi – best friends ever!

We are on our way. I have been driving for over two hours now and am kind of tired. I am behind the wheel and Mom and Mansi are sitting on the back seat. Mom has suggested at least three times already that we should stop for a tea break but there is no way that is happening – I never stop for *tea* breaks when I travel. Or for any kind of liquids for that matter. Because if one does so, one would have to pee. And since there are hardly any public toilets in our country on routes like these, it becomes terribly difficult, *most of all, if you are travelling with girls*. Mom says I have been like this since I was a kid. She says I even fainted once when we were coming back after a vacation in the summer. It was very hot that day and I refused to take any water at all. It was quite a scene she says – it was the loudest she has ever screamed.

"Aren't you tired? We should stop for a tea break," Mom says to Mansi.

Here she goes again.

I say nothing.

"Rishabh, it's ok, you won't have to stop the car and run to pee as soon as you sip the tea," Mom starts.

God! *Not in front of Mansi!*

To my utter horror, Mansi has caught what Mom just said and is exchanging inquisitive looks with Mom – I can see it all in the rear view mirror.

"It's ok," Mom says as she pats Mansi on her leg, "it's just that…"

"*Mom!*" I must stop her! *Stop her!*

"It's ok son, we all have to pee, it's totally natural," she says as if I am an eight year old.

I can see Mansi struggling to kill her laughter.

Thankfully Mom does not say anything beyond that.

We have gained some 3000 feet and the air is starting to become slightly chilly. It's a great feeling, isn't it – the feel of cold breeze against your skin? I simply love it.

I hear some rustling sounds from the back seat and then hear my Mom say,

"Here, take one both of you. It's getting chilly now and we are heading towards the mountains. Wear these caps. You don't want to catch a chill, do you?"

"*Mom, please!*"

"Keep quiet! First you don't look after yourself, then you fall sick, then I have to look after you. It's not done!"

"Mom…"

"Stop whining now!"

"Come on Rishabh, wear it. It is getting rather chilly," Mansi intervenes.

What is this? Were both of them up to some female bonding? Why would she take my Mom's side and not mine?! But to simply end the argument, I just wear the cap.

I have been driving in silence for over 15 minutes now. We have run out of topics. To end the weird air in the car, I turn the music on. It's Roxette! My all time favourite! Yes! This is so much better! *'What am I gonna do when I get a little excited a little in vain tell me?'*

I want to sing the song out loud like a total rock star but the sudden shock of what I see in front of me prevents me from doing anything like that. And before I can even panic, I hear my Mom almost scream,

"Oh my God! There is a police check post right ahead!"

Damn it! If the police are aware of Mr. Sahota's case and they find out that I am going to visit his farmhouse, they are gonna start suspecting me of things even more! But how would they know if I don't tell them? What if there has been a raid at my place and I was not found there and they have issued terrible orders against me? And damn! These stupid caps we are wearing – they would so suspect us to be terrorists!

"No one panic! No one panic!" Mom orders, "I can take care of this. Rishabh, just drive through and don't make any eye contact. They are not gonna ask you to stop. And if they do, just stop. Don't go speeding the check post – that is the worst thing to do. They are not gonna put you in jail. They have nothing against you."

Damn! I am doomed!

"And even if they do, I have big contacts. I know a lot of people out there. I could get you out in no time. Don't you worry." She sounds like a warrior with a sword and a shield in a battlefield.

I continue driving at normal speed.

We are crossing the check post now. The police officer looks at us and does nothing. We cross the check post and nothing happens.

"See, nothing happened. You guys were freaking out for no reason at all. You people just watch too many movies. It's not all true – it doesn't always happen like they show in the movies," she says coolly.

* * *

I bring the car to a halt, full of anxiety. We are there.

It is a huge building for a farmhouse. The thing looks mammoth and my architectural sense tells me that there must be at least eight rooms in this house, if not more. It's for sure gonna take all night to search the whole place. The house stands tall beyond a majestic garden and has a strong European character.

I am still observing and admiring the building when Mansi interrupts,

"Rishabh, I don't think we should park the car here."

What? If not here, then where are we gonna park it? Don't tell me that we need to go hide the car in the woods and then come back all the way walking.

"There is a rear court, we should park the car there; no one would be able to find the car there."

God! There is a rear yard too! How *big* is this place?

"You see this pavement turning around the building?" she says as she points towards the driveway that continues in front of us and curves around the building.

"Just follow that, it will lead you to the back yard," she continues.

I drive the car slowly around the building. The place looks damn mysterious. There are huge columns running up to the height of the first floor that are fatter than the thickest tree trunks I have seen. There are bay windows jutting out at various locations on the first floor. There is also a huge wheel window symmetrically set on the side wall of the building with an intricate stained glass pattern on it that overlooks the side garden.

I drive the car around the building and park it in the rear court.

* * *

We are all in the front porch. Mansi takes the keys out and tries to unlock the door. She struggles with it for a few seconds but ultimately turns to me with a frown. It's a major problem with duplicate keys – they are never accurate. I walk to the door and say,

"Wait, let me try."

Mansi steps back.

I try my hand at it but the key just doesn't budge. It does not feel like it's stuck, it feels like it's the limit beyond which it cannot turn. Then it hits me – I turn the doorknob and push the door open.

"The door was already unlocked," I say as I look at the others.

In the house

We enter the house and the first thing that hits me is that Mr. Sahota really has a thing for grandeur. I mean just look at the place – it's freaking *huge*! There is an entrance lobby, which has three doors opening onto a dining room, a living room and a drawing room each. The living room further opens onto another lobby that has a mammoth staircase that reminds me of the one they showed in *Titanic*. There is even a clock on the wall above the landing. And the kind of carvings and artwork I see all around, it's beyond impressive.

The place is really swanky. I turn around to look at Mom and Mansi. Mansi has been particularly silent since we have reached this place. She really seems troubled. Maybe I should try to comfort her a little.

"I think we should all sit for a while and just... breathe. It was quite a journey," I say.

"Yes," Mansi says. She is looking at the floor and is totally lost somewhere.

We go and sit on the sofas.

There is an awkward silence in the room and I want to break it.

"Really weird, isn't it – the door was unlocked. I just can't figure out why," I say as I look at Mansi who looks even more troubled to hear what I say.

"Mansi," I say turning to her, "It's gonna be fine, trust me. Don't worry so much."

She looks at me and takes a deep breath before she says, "Actually, there is something that I have been meaning to tell you."

* * *

"My uncle, he lives in Birmingham for most part of the year." There is tension in Mansi's voice and she avoids looking us in the eye.

"A few years back, he bought a restaurant there," she continues, "for which they had to take a loan even after putting in all the money they had."

She finally looks at Mom and me hesitantly and says, "The restaurant has not been doing that well." She gulps.

"That's ok, every business takes time to stablise. They must not feel let down by that." I want to console Mansi but Mom cuts me off.

"Rishabh, please let her talk."

After a few seconds, she starts again as the clock on the wall ticks loudly deepening a feeling of total tension in the room.

"He had been trying really hard but... he was not able to pay back the loan and now with the added interest, the figure he needs to pay back has become astronomical."

"You mean he has not been able to pay back the loan and the... bank people have sent someone to hunt him down and that is why he is missing." I jump. Mom only gives me a cold, stern look and I sit down quietly.

"I have had a hunch for a while now," Mansi continues, "with him going missing, he might be trying to... get out of one identity and make a new one to get rid of the loan."

"You mean he is..."

"Gonna start living under a new identity in a new place," she interrupts me.

I look at her confused.

"It's not that hard to do here in India. One just has to meet the right kind of people in the right way."

"But what about Mrs. Sahota?" I ask.

"He must have got plans for her."

"If that's the case, then we should not try to find him," I say as I look back at her.

She nods as she looks down at the table.

"In fact, if that's the case, I wish no one tries to find him right now," I add.

Now it all makes sense to me. This was the reason Mrs. Sahota was upset, and yet was not trying to find him. She knew what was on. I think about the whole thing for a while and then a realization hits me – I should be thankful that no one tried to frame me as the murderer for this case. I was literally forcing every kind of evidence against me at every dangerous site possible.

Suddenly a doubt starts to storm my mind – were they trying to frame me? That joke Mrs. Sahota played on me, was it a part of a plan? I have to ask Mansi.

"Mansi, the whole bedroom thing that happened with Kavita Aunty, was that planned? Was I being framed?"

"Rishabh, if they had ever tried anything like that, I would have never, ever let them do that. I don't really know why she did what she did, but there is no way in this world that I would have let them frame you for something like that... You know that."

What! That seduction act of her was actually an attempt to frame me! God! This is beyond anything that I had ever expected – she was gonna portray that I had an affair with her and that's why I killed her husband! I would have been in *jail* and they both would have started their new life! God! I am beyond enraged.

"You knew about all this and you never told me!" I exploded. This is the first time I'm really yelling loudly at her.

Just then Mom steps in. She looks me in the eyes and says, "The important thing is that they didn't do what came to their mind."

I look at her for a few seconds before I yell again, *"They tried to frame me!"*

Mom looks back at me with a serious expression on her face, dictating me to hold myself. But I can't, I simply can't.

"I just need some time to myself," I say as I storm out of the room.

* * *

It's really weird – being angry with someone when you are trapped in a place completely new to you. I mean like... what do I do? I don't want to even *see* the people who I came with because I am so *irritated* with them. I cannot just go out because I am technically *trespassing* and don't want anyone to notice that. I am just walking from one room to another in the lamest manner ever, without even knowing why I am doing it and what we are doing here anyway. If Mr. Sahota is neither kidnapped nor lost nor *murdered* and is simply hiding, then what are we doing here? We should just be heading back home. I cross the door to the dining room and as I am thinking of all this I catch a glimpse of its interiors. The room looks majestic. I just want to go inside and see the room before I go and suggest to everyone that we should leave.

It is the most royal dining room that I have ever seen. If I were still in college, I would have loved to write a paper on the tasteful and *lavish* quality of this space. The room is *massive.* Just look at the dining table – it's a magnificent 18-seater with single seats at its long ends. The chairs are so heavily carved, they look like thrones of kings. I just want to go and sit on that chair at the end and act like a king for once and give the cue to everyone to start dinner. I have always dreamt of being a king since I was a kid. I have told you about my Chamba background, right? And I am quite sure (still) that one day I am gonna be one – they are gonna find the prince of Chamba one day and crown him King.

I hold my head up high, walk straight to the chair and I am about to sit, instead I jump out of it immediately as something pokes my butt. What the hell is it? I am shocked at what I see. I must be beyond blind not to have noticed this huge bag lying on the chair when I pulled it back. But why would someone do this? Why would someone put a bag like that on the king's chair?

I put it on the table and unzip it.

Good smoking thunderous God of this world! Where the hell did this come from? I look at what's inside and I cannot move with the shock of what I see inside the bag.

It's a rich man's world

All three of us sit, gaping wide-eyed at the bag stuffed with money lying in front of us.

"What should we do?" I finally ask.

"I have been trying Kavita Aunty's number but it says out of coverage area," Mansi says.

"I think we should inform the police," Mom says and both Mansi and I look at her.

"For heaven's sake, we are already almost trespassing. If anything goes wrong here we are gonna be in *trouble*." Both of us still look at her speechless.

"Or if any of you has a better idea," she snaps.

"I am not gonna talk to the police, you call them," I say to Mom.

* * *

"Mr. Gurdeep said that he is coming but it would take him at least five hours to reach," Mom says after she hangs up the phone. "He has asked us to be alert and to avoid much activity."

It's been a really long day already, and now this. I don't know when all of this is gonna end. We sit awkwardly in silence and I can't pull my eyes away from the bag full of money lying in front of me. What would *I* do if I would ever got so much money all of a sudden? First of all, I would buy a beautiful house in the mountains somewhere, where I would go every summer. Then I would make a big 'cinema room' in my house. Where I would finally fulfill my dream of watching *Out of Africa* on a big screen. And then I would put the rest of the money in a bank or just invest it in some 'bonds' where it could grow. But I don't really need to *dream* about all of it like that because I am gonna become the King of Chamba soon and would have all the money in the world to do all I want.

Just then there is the click of the doorknob and before any of us can move or even think of anything, someone opens the door and we see Mrs. Sahota standing at the door with a bag in her hands.

All of us look at her shell-shocked. After a moment's silence (which feels like eternity), she says, "I told you not to come." Mrs. Sahota is almost on the verge of tears as she talks.

"I am really sorry but I just felt that we should help you and this was the first place that I could think of to start with, to search for clues," Mansi says.

Mrs. Sahota bursts into tears as she throws her head into her hands and starts crying. My mom walks over to her, puts her hand on her shoulder and says, "Mrs. Sahota, you are not alone in this, we all are with you. We are here to help you out. Please have faith in us, please tell us what is happening."

Recovering from a fit of sobs, she wipes her tears and says, "Someone has kidnapped Mr. Sahota." She looks at us, "Last month Mr. Sahota's great uncle passed away and left us a huge piece of land. We thought it was a blessing in disguise as with that we would not only pay off the loan we had on our heads, but also have loads of money to spare. The deal was made and we got the money. But the very next day Mr. Sahota went missing and I started to get these phone calls," she says as her eyes well up again and she falls silent.

"What calls?" I ask.

She gathers herself again and says, "Ransom calls. Some man who asked for money to release Mr. Sahota. He was to come and collect the money today. This is where he had asked me to leave the money. And he had threatened me that if I report to the police, he would... kill Mr. Sahota." She breaks off into tears again as I exchange looks with Mom realizing what we had just done.

"I kept the money in the house in the afternoon as he had asked me to, and left. But then he called again and asked for more money. I somehow arranged it and rushed back here. Please, I beg you, we all must leave. Or he will surely kill him," she pleads.

Now it all makes sense, the bag of money, why the front door was open.

"But Mrs. Sahota, this is our only chance to catch the kidnapper," I speak up, "we have to do something! We know he is gonna come here, how can we just let him go away?"

"No! You don't understand, they are very dangerous people! We *must not* mess with them," Mrs. Sahota replies instantly.

"Ma'am, I assure you, they are not gonna do anything to Mr. Sahota. Once we catch the kidnapper everything will be alright." "No!" she almost yells. "It's too risky. We have to leave the place, now!"

"But what's the guarantee that if we go and leave the money here, he would release Mr. Sahota and not ask for more money? He has already done that once," I say.

She looks at me, sitting still.

"We just have to think smartly; we just have to come up with a plan," I say.

The plan

"We need to come up with some kind of a plan," I say again, looking around at everyone.

After a moment of silence I realize that it's only me who must put his brain to test. I look around the room and suddenly an idea strikes me.

"I know!" I jump, "All of us, we wait here in this room, hiding, for the kidnapper. We switch off all the lights and wait here for him in the dark," I say as I walk to the other corner of the room where a music system is placed on a table. I turn the volume knob to the loudest and say, "And as soon as he enters the room, we flick the lights on, play some music to distract him and attack him to bring him down," I say, turning on the music system.

The song that the speakers start to blare is *Bheege hoonth tere, Pyaasa dil mera...*

I feel a strong punch of embarrassment and I can't even look anyone in the eye. I turn the music off and Mom says, "I don't think that's a good plan."

There is complete silence in the room as I look around, racking my brains to devise a plan to trap the evil kidnapper and then it strikes me!

* * *

"I think it's totally juvenile," Mom says, "We are not in a *Home Alone* movie."

She has gone into a zone where everything I say is gonna sound stupid to her.

"Come on, it will work, I know the plan will work," I say as I look at everyone around, hoping for someone to support me. Mom looks at me with total disapproval in her eyes. Mansi is looking at me blankly and I can almost hear Mrs. Sahota's thoughts say that she knew staying here was total trouble and all of us should have left this place long back.

I don't care what anyone is thinking – I totally believe in my plan 100 percent.

"And if anyone has a better plan, please come up with it," I say as everyone keeps staring at me silently.

"We still have a few hours before it gets dark. I am sure the kidnapper is not gonna come anytime soon. And there is no way Inspector Gurdeep can make it to this place in less than four hours. I really need help from all of you to catch this kidnapper."

Silence.

"Please, we are running out of time here!" I plead.

* * *

Mansi, Mrs. Sahota and I are hiding behind the bushes outside in the garden and our eyes are fixed on the front porch next to which there is this huge wheel window that opens out onto the garden.

Mom is in the garage where the distribution board for the electric supply to the house is ready for action. It is dark and we wait there for over an hour before we see a dark shadow creeping towards the porch. This is the time to gear up and *just do it.* If all goes as planned, we would have the kidnapper, Mr. Sahota, the money, all with us today.

Cautiously, the man turns the doorknob, slowly opens the door, walks inside and closes the door with an audible, crisp click. Ok, this is the time to give Mom the cue. I pull out the flashlight and in less than a second Mom turns on the power and there is light everywhere and we hear the loud siren of a police van. It's working – the sound clip that I had is playing on the music system, it's working! Now we can see the man wearing a black mask frantically trying to open all the three doors in the entrance lobby but obviously he can't as we have locked all of them. There is only one way out and that is the wheel window. It's only a matter of seconds before he runs to the window, jumps out and falls into the pit, that we had dug, with a loud thud. Ok, this is our turn to act – all three of us run to the pit and slide the heavy marble slab over it. And stand on its edges. Mission accomplished – we have trapped the kidnapper. I look at my watch, Mr. Gurdeep should be here in around 20 minutes.

The party

It was Vijay, Mr. Sahota's housekeeper, who was the kidnapper. Simple as it sounds, he got to know about the property deal that was happening and could not control his greed. He got the news in his village where he had gone to attend his brother's wedding and when he felt the time was right, he made his move. Believe it or not, he was actually keeping

Mr. Sahota in a cave in the forest. And all this time, Mr. Sahota had no idea who had kidnapped him, as he was blindfolded all the while. Now he would know what Gandhari must have felt like.

And obviously, by solving Mr. Sahota's case, we also solved the child trafficking case. The police discovered 25 children that Vijay was holding with him whom he was planning to send off to various places. Now everything is settled and I can heave a sigh of relief.

It was a huge shocker for the Sahotas but not for me. I knew from the very beginning that the guy was a criminal. It's a different thing that when Mr. Sarabjeet unmasked him, I was the first one to exclaim, "Vijay, the house keeper! I could never have imagined that!"

Where am I right now? Well, after we solved the whole case, Mr. Sahota was beyond grateful, especially to me (for what reason, I don't know – I didn't do anything great). So he decided to throw this grand party in my honour and that is where I actually am right now. And it turns out that he finally decided to go for the 'magnanimous dome' concept I generated back then for the renovation of his house. In fact, he has become such a fan of it now that he has actually got a huge dummy structure of the whole thing erected, only for this party, right above the majestic fountain in his garden. I am sitting right below it, next to the fountain, and the entire effect is totally awesome.

I turn around to look at the water fountain playfully springing up and down when I hear a voice, "Care for a coke?"

It's Mansi.

"Sure." I smile, as I take one of the two glasses she is holding in her hands.

She comes and sits next to me.

"I can't thank you enough for your help Rishabh. I don't know how things would have been without your help."

"You are welcome."

I look into her eyes and see genuine emotion. And that look, for some reason, sums up all the times that I have spent with her.

Something inside me tells me that it's time – it's time to tell her… time to confess how I have felt about her so many times in the past.

"You know, there was a time when I really started believing that I had feelings for you," I say.

She smiles and continues to look at me.

"I think I should also confess, I was also attracted to you."

Really? Me? With all my clumsiness?!

Somehow I manage to kill my thoughts and try to give a charming smile. Actually I have been thinking about this whole thing quite deeply and I have learned something from my relationship with Superna. We can't get into a relationship right now. Commitment in a relationship is too huge a promise. And I don't think we have reached that level *yet*.

"So I guess there were sparks," I say.

She smiles again.

I need to know what's on her mind – where this whole thing is going before I say anything.

"So where does that place 'us'?" I ask.

"I guess," she smiles, "We are still in the process of getting to know each other."*

It's quite a confrontation we just had. Both of us fall silent and struggle to find something to say.

"We need to..." both of us say exactly at the same time and then stop suddenly. I smile and look at her, asking her to go on.

"I think we need to start working on the classes again now. There's been quite a pause there I feel."

"That is what I was gonna say," I smile.

And at that exact moment, my phone starts to ring in my pocket. I pull it out and see the name of my school teacher flashing on the screen.

"I am sorry, but I need to take this call," I say.

"Sure," she replies.

I take the call.

"Good evening Ma'am. How are you?" It's Simran Ma'am.

"I am good, thank you. And I see that you have become quite a hero."

"Come on Ma'am." I laugh.

"Have you read the newspapers?" she says.

Actually the papers covered the story real aggressively. And for some reason, they glorified all my actions like crazy. If someone who does not know me, and does not know how everything

---

* Yess! Our minds are totally in sync! That is exactly what I think too! This is so gonna work out!

happened, reads the story, he or she would really feel that I am a hero of sorts.

"Yes, I have, and they have really exaggerated the whole thing beyond proportion," I say.

"You are never gonna change." I can hear her smile, "Anyway, that is not the only reason I called you. I have really great news for you."

"Ok."

"I am going to move to the US next month."

What? This is the *really great news* she had for me? That I don't know when I would see her again?!

"It was something I had been planning for a very long time," she continues, "And there was only one thing that was keeping me from taking the decision. I didn't want to sell the house I have here. But you just made the whole thing really easy for me."

"Is it? How?" I ask.

"I have made a trust and I want you to take care of it. I am donating my house to the trust and I want you to use the house to teach the kids there. I could never have thought of a better use for the house. And if you wish, you can use the house for boarding purposes for the kids too."

Oh my God! Am I dreaming? Is this for real? No, I can't do this, there is no way I can handle this. I just won't be able to manage it.

"Ma'am... this is huge... I can't handle this! A full set-up like that... I can't!"

"Yes, you can. We always feel that we are not ready, but when we are forced to take things in our hands, believe me, everything falls into place."

I sit there silently as my hand holding the phone almost starts to shake.

"I have to go now, I have loads to do. Things are crazy here. I will get in touch with you soon. We need to take care of quite a lot of paper work before I leave."

"Ok," I say stunned.

"Take care, see you. Bye."

"Bye" I say.

She hangs up the phone.

I see Mansi looking at me expectantly as I turn around to look at her.

"I think a lot of our problems just got solved. We are all ready to take our classes to the next level!" I say.

It all rounds off (Or does it?)

Natasha: so, how's everything going?

Rishabh: really cool actually. we managed to get all the kids freed from the 'servant jobs' they were doing. now they all live at 'The Home' (yes, that is what we are calling it). we teach the kids during the day. and in the evening, we all get together and make small paintings. mansi had some connections with some art dealers who agreed to source our work and thankfully some income has also started coming in. if all goes as planned, we would soon not only be able to support ourselves, but also make some profits.

Natasha: great!

Rishabh: yes, if all goes well, me and mansi have plans to start our own NGO soon using all this as our base.

Natasha: ☺ talking of mansi, how is she?

Rishabh: oh, she is good. and you know, she and Mom have become quite pally now. ever since we came back from that little 'adventure trip' of ours. they both have been going out for shopping and God knows what, together. they keep meeting each other without me most of the time and don't even tell me what they are up to.

Natasha: hmm, interesting. and you and mansi, where do you stand?

Rishabh: i think we are still very much in the process of getting to know each other ☺

Natasha: and your job? how did your boss react when you quit?

Rishabh: it was quite weird actually. when I went to him and told him that i would be leaving the office in two weeks' time, he just mumbled a lightly audible 'hmm' and that was it. savaray, on the other hand, created a great scene when i told him that i would be leaving office soon. so i thought it would be a good idea to take him with me. now he takes care of 'The Home' and the children during the night.

Natasha: nice.

Rishabh: it's funny in some ways, when i came here, i was so… suffocated! everyone is different now. not everyone can successfully find himself or herself at the age of 20 and know what he or she wants to do for the rest of life and get married by 24 and have kids by 27 and start taking care of everyone and so on. some people take time to find themselves. and no one has a right to treat them like outcasts… or criminals! some answers don't come easy to some people and no one has the right to hate them for that. and if you really ask me, we all keep changing throughout our lives. it's only that we never sit down and take time to understand that. we just get so stuck in the ways of the world, that we never realize that we have changed, what it actually is that we really like. going to an IIT and having an IIM degree is not the sole purpose of life for everyone. and neither should it be like that.

Natasha: true.

Rishabh: all of us want to live the safe, tried and tested life. even if it does not suit us, even if it is not meant for us. we live in boxes and in such great fear of the unknown beyond those boxes. we are supposed to take up regular jobs and do nothing beyond that. if i think about it, i should never have argued with mr. sahota about ramesh and should never have brought him home. i should have stayed in the box. and if i had done that, i would not have faced any of the complications, would never have got involved in the case and we would not have been able to catch the kidnapper. i think it's very true for most people – the fear of an unknown danger is greater than the fear of a known danger, even if the known danger is greater than the unknown danger. and that is only because it lies outside our 'box'.

Natasha: wow! great quote.

Rishabh: i know ☺

Natasha: ☺ great. so, the orange hangover finally showed its true colours.

Rishabh: ☺ i guess so.

The creative adult is the child who has survived.

— Ursula K. Le Guin

And it's time to say – Thank You!

As much as I like writing stories, I hate it when a story ends – it's so painful to accept that I will not be able to see any new antics of the characters I fell in love with while creating them. But once again I hope that you had as much fun reading the story as I had writing it.

It's not the author alone who comes up with a story, everyone around him is also involved. For if there were no inspiration, there would be no stories. So once again it's time to thank everyone who helped and inspired me to write this story.

I would like to thank my parents, my sister and my family; without their help and support, none of this would have been possible.

Mr. R.H. Sharma, Akash Shah and everyone at Jaico for believing in my work – thank you so much, a story would remain largely untold without its publisher.

Lakshmi for her valuable inputs – we all know how terribly a book reads without a good editor. Thank you.

Novoneel Chakraborty for sparing all those hours for the most exciting discussions; I just can't thank you enough for helping me with the endless re-drafting. We both know what the story would have been like if you had not helped - thank you.

Bhaskar Bhatt for his constant guidance and suggestions – really can't thank you enough.

Kamrej and Naushad Ali for making such lively and joyful

illustrations.

The Fountain Pen Guild for their presence, support, actions and suggestions – thank you so much.

Gabru Chotta Kutta Jawan for being the God-sent gift who taught me an utmost valuable lesson.

Mr. Narinder Arora, Ram Savaray, Manju and Krishna for all their inspiration, excitement and encouragement.

Guneet for always being there and for always forcing me to do the *right thing*. All my friends – Aksha, Shweta, Kunal, Pragya, Shivani, Deepali, Rajat, Varun and Sumit Kumar for always being around and putting up with my endless cribbing when I could not 'get the story right.' Thank you so much guys; life would have been so boring and dull without you.

Siddhartha Sharma for his constant motivation, encouragement and push. For what it's worth, you *have* managed to make me think differently.

Rehan Shaurya for his smart observations and suggestions.

Harkawal and Ricky for helping me on that ever critical evening – thank you, the story did change that evening.

Dolly Aunty for all those chocolate cakes and those unbelievably scrumptious meals.

Sunil Kumar for helping me with all those odd corrections – I know how painful the job must have been – thank you.

Sanjay, Shubh and Veer Singh from the Ashoka Restaurant, McLeod Ganj – thank you so much for serving me so patiently for those endlessly long hours and for filling me up with so many new stories.

Everyone from the No Name Café, McLeod Ganj and all the strangers I met there who shared their stories with me – thank you.

Anuja and all my Facebook friends for being around and for all the fun – thank you.

And most of all, I would like to thank all of my readers. It's you whom I work for; it's you for whom I write. My work would not exist without your love and support.

I hope you had a great time reading the story, Thank you!